MURDER ON THE SAANICH PENINSULA

An evocative mystery with a jaw-dropping ending

KATHY GARTHWAITE

Paperback edition published by

The Book Folks

London, 2020

© Kathy Garthwaite

This book is a work of fiction. Names, characters, businesses, organizations, places and events are either the product of the author's imagination or are used fictitiously. Any resemblance to actual persons, living or dead, events or locales is entirely coincidental. The spelling is British English.

All rights reserved. No part of this publication may be reproduced, stored in retrieval system, copied in any form or by any means, electronic, mechanical, photocopying, recording or otherwise transmitted without written permission from the publisher.

ISBN 978-1-6570-4907-9

www.thebookfolks.com

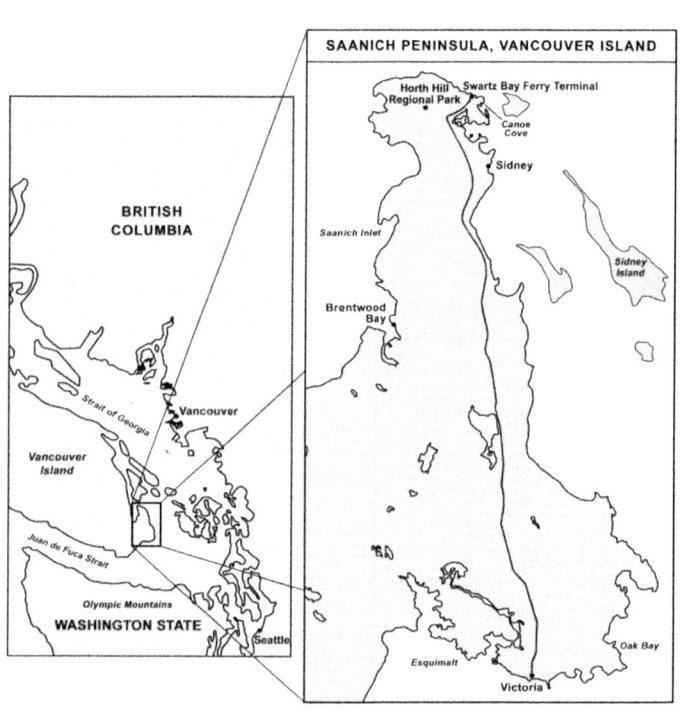

For Mom. Miss you.

Chapter 1

Ryder Simpson stood mesmerized for several minutes. He dropped his head onto his chest and brushed his fingertips against his temple. The knife in his clenched fist grew heavier, the sticky handle causing his stomach to do a flip-flop. As he stared in disbelief at the gore, the air took on an ominous tension like static lightning. Three sharp blasts from a ship sounded in the distance, and snapped him back to reality. But even so, he hesitated, powerless to steady his nerves. He wasn't sure what to do next, and then he tossed the weapon as far as he was able into the ocean.

He heard the rumble as a ferry moved astern out of its berth and lurched forward. The earth shuddered under his worn-out boots. The ship's twin screws churned up the wash into frothy bubbles as it travelled toward Active Pass on its way to Vancouver. A long-reaching swell spread out toward the once peaceful town of Sidney, and the stilled figure on the craggy shore.

Panic struck, and Ryder ran like hell.

* * *

Paula sat in the wicker chair on the veranda and wondered where her boy had gone. She feared that it was things in her past that had forced him onto the streets. Would he ever return home? There were predators out there who prowled the town, seeking out the weak and vulnerable to manipulate for their own gain. She took a deep drag on her cigarette before flicking it to the ground and crushing the butt with the toe of her shoe. She heard the sound of footsteps fading away into the still night. After a final glance down the road, she left her post and headed inside, hoping a drink would assuage her pain.

* * *

Ruth Fletcher scurried along the ill-lit walkway. Light from the condos opposite provided faint illumination in the dusk. She felt secure in this neighbourhood, but remained vigilant while taking her evening stroll. As the light faded, shadows threatened to overtake the day and offer it to people with malicious intentions. Her boss had kept her late, and now she risked the perils of the night closing in on her. No matter, her Labrador retriever needed his walk. The frisky two-year-old dog tugged on his restraint, squirming to get loose. He swerved off the pavement, heading for an interesting smell and the young girl dropped the leash to the ground before the dog could tear her arm out of its socket. The retriever halted near the water's edge. He sniffed and jumped around excitedly.

Ruth paused as her eyes adjusted to the murkiness, allowing everything to come into focus. By degrees, an outline took shape. She scrambled over the rocks and flashed the light from her cell phone onto an object, partly hidden among the bedrock outcrops – a lifeless body. Against the pallor of the lady's skin, the blood splatter on the cotton dress was a rich ruby coloration. Ruth thrust a fist to her mouth to muffle the scream. Her heart thumped rapidly, making her feel faint. She had never seen a dead person before. As Ruth called 911, she backed away, her limbs trembling uncontrollably. Despite the coolness of the concrete, she sank to the sidewalk for support. Ruth gathered the dog close to her shivering frame as she waited for help.

Chapter 2

Inspector William Gibson had a rare evening alone. His wife was out with a friend for dinner and a movie. He should have been enjoying himself, but his mind kept wandering from the words on the page. Gibson re-read the same sentence five times before he put the book face down on the coffee table. He plucked up the letter that had occupied his thoughts since its delivery that morning, but then the shrill ring of his cell phone startled him.

Policing on the southern tip of Vancouver Island overlapped between the local police force in the City of Victoria, the Royal Canadian Mounted Police in the small towns and rural areas, and the Vancouver Island Integrated Major Crime Unit. Sometimes they worked in conjunction with each other, but when Gibson's phone rang there was never any doubt that something major was in the wind. As commander of the Vancouver Island Integrated Major Crime Unit, VIIMCU, Gibson was compelled to answer. He looked at the phone and swiped the screen.

"Gibson."

"Hello, Inspector. Bad news here. We've got a body near the Bevan Fishing Pier in Sidney," the dispatcher said. "Do you know the place?"

"Yeah. It's a street over from the main drag. Right?"

"That's it. The crime scene unit is on its way."

"What about Scottie?" he asked.

"Sergeant Ann Scott Cruickshank is en route, as well."

"OK, thanks." Gibson hung up. His problem would have to wait. He thrust the letter into his upper pocket and let out an audible sigh.

Sidney was a small town on the north end of the Saanich Peninsula, thirty kilometres straight down the highway from his office in Victoria.

By the time he arrived at the crime scene, the area was swarming with police vehicles. He greeted the officers standing by the yellow tape, holding back a flock of spectators. As he worked his way down the pavement, his second in command greeted him.

"The pathologist is here." Scottie pointed to the outcrop of rock farther down the shoreline. Pinpoints of light from battery pack spotlights were set in a circle around the victim. Flashes from a camera produced intermittent brilliant spots in the darkness.

"Is it Dr. Tilly Adler?"

"Yeah."

"How did she get here so fast?"

"She lives nearby," Scottie said. "And it's a good thing she does."

Gibson tilted his head, not getting it.

"The tide."

"Right." He swept his eyes towards the water. "Who discovered the body?"

"A young girl walking her dog. An officer escorted her home earlier," Scottie said. "She was pretty rattled."

They arrived near the water's edge where Adler was waiting.

"How long has she been dead?" Gibson asked.

"Not more than a few hours. Now, that's just an estimate until after the autopsy."

"The carotid artery. She didn't have a chance," he murmured as he peered down at the body.

"No, she didn't," Adler agreed.

"What about those other cuts?"

"I will have more for you when we get her on the slab," the pathologist said. "We have to transfer her now. The tide is coming in quickly." She scrutinized Gibson with her enormous sky-blue eyes.

"That's what Scottie said."

"Come by in the morning, closer to noon. I should have everything done by then."

She signalled to two technicians hanging around in the background. They lifted her body, put it on a stretcher and left with Adler trailing behind.

"Do we know who the victim is?" Gibson turned to Scottie. He knelt to gain a better look at where the torso had been lodged in the stones.

"Dianne Meadows. We found her handbag a few metres away." Scottie flipped through her notebook. "She lives in Sidney. On the north side."

"Have you dispatched an officer to the house to inform the family?"

"Yeah, but nobody was home."

"What about the weapon? Was that recovered?"

"It's probably in the drink." Scottie pursed her lips.

"We'll get a dive team out at first light," Gibson said as he contemplated the challenge. "Was there a cell phone in her purse?"

"No, but it could easily have fallen out. There are lots of nooks and crannies in these rocks to get jammed into. I asked the crime team to come back in the morning when they could actually see something," Scottie said as she stepped off the treacherous rocks. "Although it could be in the water with the knife."

After they were both on firm ground, they walked back to their vehicles.

"This isn't the first stabbing in Sidney," Scottie said. "My friend in the local dispatch said there has been an uptick in street robberies by teenagers. Well, that and the other disreputable people. You know the snatch and run kind. And a few knifings thrown in here and there."

"Is that right?" Gibson shook his head.

"But this is the first fatal stabbing. I hope it's not a sign of more to come." She studied her partner. "It's not a sleepy town anymore."

Gibson grunted something unintelligible. Seemingly he had other thoughts.

Chapter 3

"I was worried." Katherine glimpsed up from the morning paper she was reading and gave her husband a look.

"I left you a…" Gibson paused and flashed a silly grin. "I forgot. Sorry. It was a late call for an incident in Sidney."

"A murder by the pier." Katherine tapped the newspaper. She still enjoyed the printed page.

"The vultures."

"Do the public need to worry?" she asked.

"No."

"So, it was the husband." Katherine got up and refilled her coffee mug. She twisted around and smirked at him.

"Don't try to weasel anything out of me. You know I can't talk about it," Gibson said and changed the topic. "Did you guys have fun last night?"

"Very much so, but I'm going to stay in and rest for the day."

"That would be a sensible idea," Gibson said. He stood up and rubbed her belly. "Take care of our little guy."

Gibson touched his suit pocket with the damning letter tucked in deep. Should he mention something now? Was it a suitable time? As he wrestled with his thoughts, Katherine said something that halted him in his tracks.

"How exciting that your first child is on its way." She offered him a peck on the cheek and sat back down. "My ankles are swollen."

Gibson extended his fingers through his lush hair and decided to leave that skeleton in the closet.

"Don't wait up for me," he said. "And get lots of rest."

"All right." Her voice grew bubbly. Her skin glowed in that special way.

* * *

The inconspicuous building of the major crime unit, VIIMCU, was located on Dallas Road. The unit had its own forensic identification section where fingerprints, DNA, hair, fibres, and photographic evidence were processed. The front entrance had no signage to reveal its government designation. There were no interview rooms or cells to hold suspects, that was all done at either Victoria or Sidney RCMP detachments, depending on where the crime took place.

Gibson's office was on the second floor with a great view of mountains and water from the large corner windows. The squad met for orientation in Gibson's office after nine that morning. DC Blake Gunner and DC Danny Na were seated in front of the sizeable desk that dominated the room. Gibson sat across from the detective constables. Scottie leaned on the windowsill with her back to the ocean vista. She gazed at a photograph of the victim taken at the crime scene pinned to the incident board.

This was the first time the inspector had put up the board in his office. It was usually in the conference room down the hallway. But more often than not, the team ended up hanging out in his space. It was a comfortable room with good natural lighting, plenty of chairs, and a coffee machine on the sideboard where they could help themselves to a cappuccino or a sweet tea. So it was a sensible move to switch meetings to this office, and if nothing else Gibson was a sensible man.

The inspector sat at his desk with a slim folder in front of him and a pen in his hand. He tapped the file sharply to draw their attention away from the small talk to the investigation at hand.

"Listen up, everybody. As you know, a body was found down by the fishing pier last night. Her name is Dianne Meadows, and she lives in Sidney, not all that far from the crime scene. The victim was stabbed several times and left to bleed out. We don't have the murder weapon yet, but we believe it may have been tossed into the ocean. A dive team has been dispatched early this morning to comb the bay."

Gibson paused to consider how to say the next thing on his mind without causing a rift with Scottie. She had made it clear last night that she thought the incident was brought about by a gang of teenagers on the prowl. It had maybe begun as a robbery, but swiftly turned into a fatal stabbing.

"Okay, here's the deal. We all know that the husband is a prime suspect in a case like this."

Gibson held up his hand to ward off the protest coming from Scottie. She threw him a meaningful glance, but kept her mouth shut. He adjusted his tie and continued.

"So, we will be looking at the husband thoroughly. No doubt about that. But to be fair, Scottie's idea that the street kids may be involved is a valid point." He turned to his sergeant. "Everything we find out will go on the incident board. The facts will lead us to the killer."

Scottie pressed her lips into a suitable grin.

Gibson looked up from his notes satisfied that he had smoothed things out with his partner. They had worked together for several years now, and she knew more about him than even his wife. She knew about his first marriage and his trouble from his work trip back east last month.

Many things that he didn't share with anyone else; personal matters that he would prefer to keep private. Outside of the job, their friendship was important to him. He wanted to keep it that way.

"So, first things first. We need to round up some witnesses." Gibson chortled to himself – as if you could just go out there and find someone who had seen the whole thing. It was never that easy. And how reliable were witnesses anyway? When one person would swear the guy was thin, the other person would insist that they were fat. Regardless, they had to follow protocol. Sometimes they got lucky. He turned back to face Na.

"Could you and Gunner get out there and knock on some doors?"

"You bet," he responded.

"And Na…"

The DC looked up, his penetrating brown eyes directed at Gibson.

"…keep your eye on the divers and report their progress to me right away. The murder weapon has to be found." Gibson pictured the crime scene and added, "Go up on the pier, as well. Maybe a regular there saw something. Although, it would make more sense to visit later in the evening."

"All right. We can do that."

"Nobody was home at the Meadows' place last night, so Scottie and I will head over there first."

Gibson stood up.

"It was in the papers this morning," Scottie said. "That's not right. I hope they don't read about it in the news before we get there."

"How unfortunate," Na said. "How did that happen?"

"I'm not sure. Someone with a big mouth must have recognized the victim when they transported her to the morgue," Gibson said. "It was a large, late-night crowd for such a little town."

Gunner snickered behind his hand. The inspector threw him a warning. The constable had had a wobbly beginning in the major crime unit owing to his shenanigans. Eventually, he had shifted gears and become a valuable member of the team. But every once in a while, the rascally behaviour surfaced. Gunner and Na vacated the room quickly, feeling slightly abashed.

"Well, we better get a move on," Scottie said as she pushed away from the window.

They made their way out of the building to Scottie's vehicle.

"Where to, boss?"

Gibson rambled off the address and sat back in his seat to reflect on his problem. His mobile phone rang almost immediately.

"Gibson."

"I read about the murder," Police Chief Rex Shafer said.

The inspector cringed and disregarded the jab.

The chief worked out of the RCMP detachment on Caledonia Street in Victoria. He had lots of opinions. For the most part, he left them alone to carry out their job, but he was a stickler for being kept in the loop. After all, he was the supervisor of the major crime unit above Gibson and had to deal with public sentiment. The boss was all political and didn't relish the fact that the story had leaked to the papers.

"The victim was stabbed," Gibson said.

"Any ideas yet who did this?"

"It's too soon."

"All right. Keep me posted." Rex hung up.

"Is he going to be a problem?"

"Only if a street person did it," Gibson said.

"Why's that?"

"Because that means the townspeople will be fearful of the street?" Gibson raised an eyebrow.

Chapter 4

The north side of town consisted of narrower streets and smaller dwellings than the south end but had pleasant gardens. Scottie pulled up to the curb in front of an old split-level house. The roof was covered with moss, and the white stucco was stained with rusty streaks at the corners due to malfunctioning gutters. The curtains were pulled wide open, showing spotted windows. Dandelions had taken over a front lawn that had died to a brownish-yellow mass from lack of water. A newer pickup truck sat in a driveway that had the same moss finding a home in the cracks that ran in patterns along its length.

They stood on the porch to gather their wits. This was the most dreadful part of the job, having to deliver the bad news. It was extremely strenuous on Scottie when kids were involved. Her sister with her two adolescent daughters remained the only family she had left. Although they didn't know if Dianne had any children, it was a real possibility. No matter what the circumstances were, the horror of murder hit the people left behind. Gibson gave a sideways glance to Scottie and rang the doorbell.

A gangly, slender man in his forties wearing polyester pants and a worn plaid shirt swung open the door. He had thick, dark hair, with a few flecks of grey on the crown, that he brushed forward to cover a pockmarked face. But what startled Scottie was the anger radiating from his eyes. She took a pace backward and automatically placed her hand on her gun.

"Did you forget your keys? Where the..." he paused. "Who the hell are you?" His lips curved into an ugly leer.

"Mr. Meadows?" Gibson said.

"Yeah. I'm Kevin Meadows." He gave them a once over, his angry outburst abating when he realized who they might be. "You're the police. Did my wife get into an accident or something?"

"I'm Inspector Gibson. This is my partner, Sergeant Cruickshank. May we come in for a moment?"

"You can tell me here," he said, barring entrance into the home. His irritation had subsided, but was unrelinquished.

"Dad, is it Mom?" A teenage girl with long fair hair and a ring in her nose ran up behind her father and pushed him aside.

"I'm sorry, but we have some bad news. Your wife was found dead last night. She was murdered," Gibson said. Straight out was usually the best way. "Sorry for your loss," he added over the hysterical scream that had erupted from the daughter. She leaned awkwardly into her dad.

"My Dianne? Are you sure? It can't be." His mouth flapped open. The bluster had faded completely, along with his rosy complexion.

"We would like it if you could come down to identify her," Gibson said.

The girl shrieked and burst into tears.

"Virginia. It's okay." He placed his arm around her shoulder and dragged her inside. Without a backward glance, he yelled out, "You better come in. And shut the door."

The detectives followed Kevin down the hallway to a bright and pleasant room. Through a large window, they could see a pie-shaped backyard surrounded by a high fence. A massive table dominated the kitchen—definitely the focal point of life for this household. Its surface was scarred with nicks and dents from heavy use, but had the radiance of well-polished wood. Eight chairs set in place had flowered cushions on the seats that matched the drapes. Virginia sat down with a thump and continued to cry, big giant tears that made her eyes well up. She paused to suck in mouthfuls of air and wept some more. Her chin trembled like an adolescent child, not like the unruly teenager that she was. Kevin sat beside her and tucked her in close, rocking her in a gentle motion.

"I don't understand. Who would want to harm Dianne?" Kevin glowered at one detective to the other with disbelief and choked out his next question. "Where?"

"By the Bevan Fishing Pier."

"That's one of her favourite spots. She goes down there all the time to watch the crabbers. Only she wouldn't be there at night. I thought she was at a baby shower. What the hell is going on?" Kevin asked. An expression of bemusement crossed his face as if he had forgotten where he was or who he was.

Gibson waited to enable the man's reality to catch up with his thoughts. After a time, he inquired, "Where was this party?"

"I don't know. Somewhere in Sidney," he snapped. "It wouldn't be on the pier."

"Who could we ask?" Gibson waited for the man to settle down. It was something he had gotten used to. It started with denial and quickly moved to anger. The bargaining, depression, and acceptance were the parts of the framework that came after.

"Someone at her work would know," he said. "Yeah, somebody there would know for sure. She's the loan manager at the Canada Trust branch."

Scottie wrote down everything in her notebook. She waited with a hand poised over the page for the next question she knew was coming.

"Where were you last night?" Gibson tried saying it without levelling an accusatory finger in Kevin's direction. The man would be in anger mode for quite a while. It appeared as if he lived his life in a rage, so he wasn't surprised at the response that came immediately.

"You, bastard. Coming in here and accusing me of murdering my wife," he screamed. "In front of my kid. Can't you see how this has distressed her? What is the matter with you?" He hit his fist on the table.

Virginia seemed immune to his rage, so lost was she in her grief.

Gibson remained quiet while Kevin let off some steam. Scottie kept her head down and pretended she was busy writing something. The worst of the explosion would blow over. Give him a minute or two.

"I would never hurt my wife," he said. "Are you sure it's her?"

Gibson waited patiently as the man bounced back to denial.

"I work at the Swartz Bay ferry terminal in the maintenance section. That's where I was last night." His eyes narrowed into dark slits as suspicion of the detective's motives whirled in his head. "My shift began at eight. I can prove it."

"We only have a few more questions, and we'll be on our way."

"How did she die?" His voice came high-pitched and cold.

Gibson knew the question was imminent, but he didn't want to describe the methods the killer had used, not with the young girl in the room. She was already in a tizzy. The details were quite shocking, even to the detectives. He lowered his head slowly.

"I asked you, how did Dianne die?" Kevin glared at the investigator. His voice had levelled, but a hint of aggression lay below the surface.

"She was stabbed with a knife."

Virginia let out a deep gasp.

"God damn it. It was those punks. Wasn't it? It's been in all the papers." He slammed his fist on the table more forcibly this time.

Gibson ignored the flare-up and continued, trying to gain the daughter's attention. "Where were you last night? Nobody answered the door when the officers came to tell you what had happened." He leaned toward her with a sympathetic expression on his face.

Virginia peered up with inflamed eyes that didn't blink.

"Why didn't you answer the door?" Kevin demanded.

The crying had eased into a measured quick intake of breath and a slow puff of air. "I guess I was asleep. I didn't go out last night." Her eyes darted around the room as if she had more to say. Instead, she clamped her mouth shut and stood up. Her face was a picture of devastation, but something flashed in her eyes. And as quickly, it retreated.

Gibson threw his partner a glance. Had she seen the hesitation? What did the girl know?

"We'll keep in touch. We're sorry for your loss," Gibson said again as he stood up to leave.

"Find the person who did this to us," Kevin snarled.

The detectives walked down the path to their vehicle.

"The girl knows something," Gibson said.

"What? You think she's in cahoots with her dad to kill her mother?" Scottie asked.

"It's possible Virginia witnessed something," Gibson replied.

"I suppose. If it was Kevin?"

Gibson did think it was Kevin. He didn't like the guy. He had a temper that was scary. It wasn't the first time the detective had seen this kind of behaviour. He thought back to a case he had dealt with a number of years ago – a missing woman that was eventually found cut into pieces. The husband had been on the cable networks pleading for the police to find her, to get the person responsible. He had the crocodile tears, and the breakdown in front of the camera over the loss of his wonderful wife. At the beginning, the family gathered round him in support. But in the end, he was outed as the monster that Gibson thought he was all along.

Chapter 5

The morgue was located at the rear entrance of Vic General Hospital. It was a place that you went to and left in a rush. It held no attraction for the detectives, especially for Scottie. As far as she was concerned, it never got any better regardless of the number of times she had been there. It even became worse as time passed by, knowing what to anticipate. So, she braced herself and followed Gibson into the bleak room with her body held tight.

Dr. Tilly Adler was seated on a stool, her stubby legs dangling in the air, peering down a microscope. She hopped to the ground, greeting them in a cordial manner. In a somewhat absent-minded way, she pushed her glasses back up onto the bridge of her nose. At that point, she moved over to a stainless table in the middle of the room.

"Right on time. There's a lot to cover."

The detectives stood across from the pathologist and studied Dianne's exposed body. Scottie shivered.

"If you observe her neck on the left side, you can see where the knife entered. It hit her carotid artery," Adler began. "Death would have been practically instantaneous. There are three more stab wounds in the chest. They were post-mortem as if the person struck her again right away."

She stole a glance toward Gibson, her eyes widened. "There was no need. She was already gone by then. Makes me think it was personal."

"What caused that? Is it part of the stabbing?" Gibson pointed to some bruising along her breast.

"No. This lady has several areas of bruising in various stages of healing over her entire body. This one appears to be more recent like someone had punched her hard," Adler said, pointing to a yellowish mark. "And she has received more than her fair share of fractured bones."

"What are you implying?" Gibson asked.

"I'm telling you that these injuries are typical of a victim of domestic abuse. Her injuries are in places that are usually covered by clothing. That's to hide the apparent signs of violence."

"We've met the husband, so I'm not surprised," Gibson said.

"That's not for me to say." Adler peered over her glasses and studied the detectives.

"But it sure is a reasonable place to start," Gibson said. "Kevin was real quick to anger when we spoke with him earlier. In my mind, he appeared to be your classic abuser. We could use this information to pressure him more."

"Oh. There's one other matter," Adler said.

"What's that?"

"She was pregnant."

"Oh, my God!" Scottie exclaimed. "That's dreadful."

"Thanks, Tilly." Gibson said, keeping any thoughts of a baby to himself.

"No problem. I'll write up my report and forward it over."

The investigators left the morgue, but the chill followed them out of doors. They walked down the sidewalk soaking in the warmth of the sun. The sounds of ordinary people setting about their business surrounded them.

"Well, there's motive now. Maybe even opportunity."

"I don't know, Gibson. The guy was at work. He has an alibi."

"He says he was at work, but he could be lying. We haven't checked that out yet."

"That's right, we haven't. I don't think it's a good idea to jump to conclusions."

"For all we know, he has a girlfriend as well," Gibson said.

"We need evidence before dragging him in. Just because he might have been beating his wife, doesn't mean he killed her. And not just that, but I really think the bad-asses on the streets are the culprits. Don't you?" Scottie glanced at him before she pulled away from the curb.

Gibson could tell she was ticked off with him for being so dogged. The exchange with his partner had flustered him. When did he get so narrow-minded? Why was he desperately anxious to accuse the husband?

A drop of rain hit the windshield. Within seconds, a torrential downpour started. It hammered on the roof like a hail of bullets and bouncing off in all directions.

"Where did that come from?" Scottie gawked at a gloomy cloud whistling across the sky.

"Let's visit Dianne's workplace and speak to her colleagues," Gibson said. "Sorry, Scottie. I can be such an ass."

"Forget it. I know that case a few years ago got under your skin. We have a long way to go before this gets solved."

She leaned forward with her eyes squinted, trying to see through the wipers that whipped at warp speed. They were hardly a match for the quantity of rainfall. The tires hissed on the blackened roads as she drove back to Sidney. The rain fell steadily, and then disappeared as quickly as it had started.

Chapter 6

The bank was on the corner of Beacon and Fifth Street. Every parking space along the street was occupied. Scottie had circled the block a few times before she noticed customer parking in the back of the bank building. The rainfall had left deep puddles that created obstacles for the detectives as they worked their way to the rear entrance. Gibson turned at the sound of a vehicle hitting a deep pool of water on the road and as a result, stepped into a puddle. The dampness leaked into his shoes immediately.

"Damn."

Scottie just laughed it off.

The lobby had white marble floors, subdued lighting, large vases of fresh-cut blossoms, and a row of clocks on the back wall displaying local time around the globe. Gibson approached the receptionist at the front counter. The man's black suit was tailor-made, fitting a trim physique. The crisp clean shirt was complemented by a silver and black tie. His hair was flawless, not a cowlick sticking up or a lock dangling into his grey eyes.

"How may I assist you?"

"May we have a moment with the manager? It's official business." Gibson produced his badge.

The man reached over, picked up the phone and punched in a number. The manicured nails with a French polish seemed entirely suitable for the job. After the receptionist hung up, he gestured to a line of chairs opposite. "He'll be right out."

"Thanks." Gibson turned to sit but was distracted by a disturbance to his left. A well-dressed lady hurried from an office, scurried down a hallway and out of view.

"What was that all about?" Scottie asked.

"Who knows? Maybe she's overdue for lunch." Gibson shrugged and looked at one of the clocks. "An extremely late lunch."

"Speaking of which, I'm famished. We didn't get any lunch today." Scottie placed her palm to her head and feigned being dizzy from lack of nutrition. "And I could use an extra-large coffee."

"That'll be our next stop."

A burly man hastened over to them.

"Good afternoon, detectives. I'm Jackson Parker. How may I serve you?"

The manager was dressed in a suit of fine summer wool, a sombre shade of azure. The tie was a paler blue with a diamond stick pinned in the centre. He wore his thinning hair short, held into place with a sandalwood scented gel. Everything perfect, except for the watermarks on his suede shoes.

Gibson stared down at his own soggy shoes and grinned sheepishly.

"May we speak in private?"

"By all means, my apologies. This way." He pointed to the office that the young lady had left only minutes earlier.

It was a substantial room befitting a director of a national bank. The walls were decorated with various diplomas and certification from the most reputable academic institutions in the country—McGill and Queen's University. The files, layered in messy piles on the desktop, were strangely at odds with its gleaming surface. Nestled among the papers was a wedding picture in a gilded frame. The lady was willow-wand thin with a shallow, pale face and dull eyes. Compared to the rugged square chin of her husband and his deep ocean green eyes, the couple were quite a contrast to each other; in appearance anyway. Who knew about their thoughts?

Gibson pulled his gaze from the picture and blushed when he realized the manager was regarding him closely.

A roguish smirk passed over Jackson's lips momentarily, and then it took flight. It was superseded by the grave expression most people expect from a banker. "That's my wife. Of twenty years. Are you married, detective?"

"Indeed, but not as long as that."

Scottie shook her head.

"Well, have a seat." Jackson pointed to the chairs in front of his desk.

"We have some bad news to report."

"Really? I can't imagine."

"It's about Dianne Meadows," Gibson said.

"It's her day off."

"I'm very sorry, but Mrs. Meadows is dead."

"What? Are you sure?" He sought the room for somewhere to fasten his eyes on. They landed on the wedding photo.

"Yes, we are."

"Was it a car accident or something? Surely, not a heart attack. She's way too young for that."

"She was murdered."

"Oh, my God! How? Who?" Jackson sputtered over his questions and rubbed at his chin. "I can't believe it." He pushed back into his seat and wiped his brow.

Before Gibson could utter anything more Jackson asked, "How is Kevin bearing the news?"

"It's what you would predict. He's in shock."

"And Virginia? Oh, dear!"

"She's not taking it well. It's very hard on her. Losing her mom."

"What can I do?" Jackson asked. He surveyed the detectives.

"When was the last time you saw Mrs. Meadows?" Gibson asked, choosing to ignore the question.

"Dianne worked until about six yesterday. She was the last person out beside me, of course. I was here quite late working on a project." Jackson peered at his gold watch. "I don't mean to rush you, but I have a meeting across town to get to."

"All right, just a few more questions," Gibson said. "We understand she was the loans manager. What can you tell us about her work? Any client problems?"

"Absolutely not," Jackson said. "All above board. She was much loved and respected by everyone. Her clients. Her fellow colleagues. There's nothing to see here. Nothing."

"We would like to speak to each member of staff," Gibson said as he stood up. "Just briefly. If you could arrange that?"

"To be sure, use my office. It's more private." With that, Jackson headed to the receptionist and after a moment returned.

"It's all arranged. I must be on my way now. It's a terrible tragedy."

"Much appreciated."

Jackson picked up his various folders, jammed them into a briefcase and left. The detectives talked to each employee in turn. Nobody had encountered Dianne after work on Thursday. One young woman had been invited to the baby shower but hadn't been able to make it. She gave them the name and number of the hostess.

Everybody seemed to like Dianne, although apparently she was a very reserved person. Agreeing to go to the shower was a bit out of character for her, as she typically avoided crowds. But there were no negative comments made about this soft-spoken lady. Nothing untoward. Dianne was just a normal everyday working mom.

As soon as they stepped outside, Scottie said, "Let's grab that sandwich now." The clouds had dispersed. The puddles in the parking lot had evaporated by the heat of the sun. It had turned into a lovely sunny afternoon. They got into the vehicle. Scottie started up the engine.

A sharp rap on the glass startled Gibson. It was a young lady from the bank. He rolled the window down. She stood there, her fingers tugging at the sleeve of her jacket. Her eyes were filled with anguish. He waited for her to say something.

"I think Dianne was having troubles at home." She spoke in a subdued voice, glancing back at the doors.

"What kind of problems?"

"You know. Family." She swallowed hard. "I shouldn't have mentioned anything." She moved away and fled back inside before Gibson could ask anything else.

Chapter 7

A faint breeze coming off the ocean blew along Beacon Avenue where Scottie, once again, hunted for a place to park. Gibson kept his window open and breathed in the fresh salt air. She pulled in front of a pizza joint and shut off the engine.

"This is the closest I can get. Not much closer than we were a minute ago."

"No problem. Can I buy you a beer and a slice instead of a sandwich?" He peeked at his watch. "It's nearly time to go home."

"You said it."

The restaurant wasn't very busy at all. A group of women, laughing and gossiping, were crowded together in a corner stall. Two lovebirds were in another, holding hands and sipping white wine as they gazed into each other's eyes. The waiter came with a menu straight away and rambled off the specials. They ordered and sat back to consider the day.

"So, what was that girl's name that just spoke to us outside?" Gibson asked.

"Was it Chelsea?" Scottie pulled out her trusty notebook and scanned the pages. "Yup. Chelsea Stone. She's the head teller."

"She knew about the shower and handed us the contact number. But she didn't go?"

"That's right. She couldn't make it." Scottie peered at the waiter who dropped off two mugs of beer and a pizza. "Thanks."

"What do you think she meant about trouble at Dianne's home? Was she privy to the domestic violence going on there?"

"We haven't any confirmation of domestic violence in the home. Dianne could be one of those accident-prone people." Scottie rolled her eyes.

"It seems like a logical conclusion to me."

"Perhaps so, Gibson. Only, we can't just be spouting out accusations without any proof."

"I'll get Na to check out the hospital records. And we should have another chat with Chelsea. It's possible Dianne confided things to her. You know, someone to share your sorrows with."

"Okay. That's reasonable."

"Wow. Now I'm reasonable."

Scottie poked him on the shoulder. "You have been prickly lately. I didn't want to say, but is there a problem with Katherine or the baby or..."

"No. Nothing like that." Gibson patted his pocket and felt the letter. "I'll tell you later."

They finished up their snack and walked to the waterfront. A truck parked along the boulevard close to the rock outcrops had a diver's emblem, a red and white flag, painted on its side panel. There were several men standing around with wet suits pulled down to their waist. The detectives walked under the yellow tape and approached the crime scene. Gibson didn't know these guys and produced his badge. They shook hands and introduced themselves.

"Where are Gunner and Na?"

"They left hours ago."

"Have you uncovered anything yet?"

"No. Nothing. But there are two divers still in the water." He contemplated the gigantic instrument on his wrist. "They'll be up in ten minutes. Tops."

"We'll wait."

"It'll be the final dive for the day. Do you want us back tomorrow, if the last guys come back empty?"

"We'll see." Gibson shrugged. The detectives walked out onto the rocks and scanned the area. "Na would have called if they discovered anything here?"

"Sure he would."

They wandered around aimlessly, staring down into dark crevices. There were pools of water with tiny crabs trapped in the hollows carved out by the constant motion of the ocean. Some contained starfishes waiting for the tide to liberate them. Gibson looked out into the small cove. He knew an artificial reef made of hollow concrete spheres surrounded the pier and attracted divers from all around. Only today the area was roped off as part of the crime scene, and the divers had been turned away.

Gibson felt the sting of a cool wind on his cheek. The breeze had rallied in the last few hours, blowing down Haro Strait, bringing a chill to the salty air. A few boats at anchor bobbed in the waves, tugging on their lifelines. The choppy water broke around the rocks in the shallows. As the tide rolled in, they disappeared beneath the surface. Closer to shore, Gibson noticed the two divers as they emerged from the sea, an object in the hand of the diver nearest to him. Had they recovered something?

The men clambered over the rocky shoreline and headed to the truck. The detectives followed them as quickly as they could, hoping for the best. The man in charge turned around when Gibson approached.

"Did you find something?" Gibson asked.

"Just a bunch of junk. No knife." He held up the bag for the detectives to see.

"Okay, thanks for all your help."

"Should we come back tomorrow?"

"No. It was a long shot."

As the divers packed up their equipment, the detectives wandered along the beach at the high tide mark to discuss what to do next.

"We need the murder weapon," Scottie said.

"Definitely."

They walked for a good stretch along the rocky shoreline before turning back, all the while scanning the ground in hopes of finding something. Before the sinking sun disappeared behind the distant hills, its final rays of light lingered in the sky. A quick flash caught Gibson's eye. He found himself looking down at a knife jammed tightly into a crevice.

"Holy shit," Gibson said. "Did we just find the murder weapon?" He put on some latex gloves and pulled the object from its hiding place. It was a single-edged knife with a groove on its thin blade. The handle had no wear on the varnish, practically brand new. And, it was smeared with a dried patch of brown.

"It has to be. That's blood," Scottie said. "Let's pray there are prints, as well.

Chapter 8

At first, Ryder had run through the side streets and looped back to the hostel that was housed in a building beside the skate park. Everything he owned was in his backpack in a locker in the back room. Did he dare walk right in and collect it? He decided to wait it out and sat on the uppermost ridge of the cement rink instead.

The lights that usually shone on the park had shut off an hour ago. He was just another shadow against the grey backdrop. It wasn't the first time he had sat there and contemplated life. And it wasn't the first time he wished he had a cigarette to occupy his hands. But money was limited, and if he begged for a smoke now, he would expose himself unnecessarily. Better to stay hidden until he could figure out what to do next.

As a result he sat there, crunched into as small a figure as he could, to observe the entrance of the hostel, striking his hands nervously on his thighs. So far there hadn't been a great deal to see. No flurry of activity. No police came. But time was quickly running out. The doors would shut at midnight until seven the following day. He watched as the last of the daytime staff left the building. With only one attendant on the night shift, he made his move.

As nonchalantly as he could, Ryder strolled into the building past the admission window. A quick peep over told him that Stud was still in the back brewing a pot of coffee to keep himself awake into the small hours of the morning. He hurried to the washout area and cleaned up as fast as he could. He twirled the lock and retrieved his pack. Nobody had spotted him yet, so he crept down the hallway to make his escape. That's when his luck ran out.

"Hey, Ryder. Not staying the night?" Stud shouted at him.

Damn. Ryder threw him a wave and sped out the door back to his observation post on the upper side of the rink. He had been on the street for a few weeks now and was used to the push and pull of the old-timers. It was the newer, younger crowd that he dreaded. They were into drugs, and scuffles were the norm. Usually he could deflect them. But when he couldn't, his trusty knife was his ally. The speed weasels almost peed themselves at the sight of the razor-sharp blade and would scowl and flee. Only after the struggle with Dianne, all he had left now were his bare hands to defend himself, and that wasn't enough. Ryder lay his head on his backpack and stared up at the stars. Before long his eyes grew heavy, and he fell asleep.

Ryder woke up with a start, but didn't move a muscle. Was it a threat? He held his breath, but the only sound he heard was the twittering of birds. No stealthy footsteps scraping up the steep incline for a surprise attack. As he sat up, the first ray of light flashed in his eyes, intensified by its path across the smooth ocean water. The sunlight warmed his cold body with just his jacket to shelter him from the dew that had formed in the early hours.

Even as Ryder pulled his knees up to his chest into a tight ball, he realized the jacket would have to go. He rifled through his pack to see how much cash he had left. A coin slipped from his fingers and rolled down the embankment of the skate rink, spiralling into a perfect landing at the bottom. He fetched the coin and split. As Ryder walked away, he tore off his jacket and searched for a bin in which to discard it. But something cautioned him to dispose of it farther afield, so he kept walking toward the town centre. It wasn't long before he found a dumpster at a construction site and pitched it into the rubble, never to be seen again.

Ryder felt a bit disoriented from lack of food, and probably from fear as well. He stepped into a fast-food restaurant and grabbed a coffee and a breakfast sandwich. It seemed prudent to keep moving, so he ate while he walked and thought about his quandary. Ryder felt better after getting some food in his growling belly, seeing as he hadn't eaten for almost a day. At that point, it dawned on him that if the knife wasn't recovered, he would be free and clear from the whole mess. He headed down to the bay, deciding to hang out on the pier or in some spot where he would be unnoticed. When he got there, a dive team was already in search of the weapon. Ryder spent the day, coming and going from the crime scene, trying to remain invisible. It was late in the day when they retrieved the knife. Not from the water but from the shore. He was screwed.

Ryder took off to find himself a place to hide.

Chapter 9

The empty building made Gibson's footsteps echo as he climbed up the marble steps to his office. His uncluttered desk wouldn't remain that way for long. It was only a matter of time before the paperwork stacked up as their investigation went on. He pulled out the letter that had found a home in his pocket since its arrival and slipped the note from its envelope. The embossed paper had a rich feel under his fingertips. The handwriting was bold with strong vertical lines. Gibson perused the letter before his team showed up. It posed a dilemma that he didn't need right now—with the new homicide case and a baby on its way. If nothing else, a phone call was in order. What would he tell Katherine? A gentle knock on the door broke his concentration.

"Hey." Scottie sat down and placed a folder on the edge of the desk.

Gibson put the letter into his pocket.

"What's that?" Scottie regarded him with suspicion.

"Nothing."

"I printed out all I could find about the rash of robberies. I only included muggings at knifepoint." She pushed the folder across the desk.

A thumping noise of boots resonated in the hall as the two constables made a mad dash up the steps. Gunner leaned on the door frame waiting for Na to catch up. The thin scar on the side of his face stood out pale against his flushed skin. His nut-brown hair was cut shorter than usual, although the long bangs still covered his brow. He grinned that lopsided sneer that Gibson was becoming endeared to. Na came to a halt beside Gunner, his shoes squeaking on the polished floors. He wore jeans and a tee shirt today instead of his pressed pants and open-neck shirt. His weekend outfit, work or no work.

"Gentleman. Have a seat," Gibson said. "How did it go yesterday? Find any witnesses?"

"We went to see the divers first as you requested, but..." Na started.

"Sorry, I should have called you. We found a knife later on in the afternoon. It was stuck in a crevice above the high-water mark," Gibson said. "It's at the laboratory. We'll see what happens next. I think it's the murder weapon. I'm hoping it is."

"All right. We were pretty busy canvassing the neighbourhood. There are three condo buildings along the waterfront near the crime scene. Gunner and I split up so we could get to each apartment." He smirked at his partner. "Luckily for us, this town has plenty of seniors. So most people were home."

"And?" Gibson leaned back in his chair. There was no making this go any faster.

"The people in the back of the building didn't witness anything at all. Most of them with a view at the front had gone to bed by nine." Na shrugged. "We tracked down two people who gave us some information. Maybe it will help. A man on the first floor said he heard a commotion around nine-thirty. His window overlooks the rock outcrops, but unfortunately there isn't much light that way, so he didn't actually see anything. He grumbled about how the old biddies had complained about light shining in their windows. Consequently, the council removed several lamps and switched to lower wattage with the rest. He said the witches should get drapes. So that was that."

"I talked to the other person," Gunner said. He spread out his notebook and read verbatim.

Gibson marvelled how Gunner could read the scrawl. It made him think of the tidy handwriting in the letter he had received. His mind trailed off to his problem.

"She said..."

"What was that?" Gibson snapped back to the conversation.

"What?" Gunner asked.

"Could you say that again?"

"Mrs. Lambert lives on the second floor in a corner suite. She has a good view right onto the sidewalk and over to the crime scene. She turned off her television when she heard a scream. She pushed her sliding door open, just a crack so her cat couldn't escape, and listened. But there was nothing more. She thought it was probably a seagull." He paused as he referred to the page. "As she was sliding the door closed, she heard someone running along the sidewalk." Gunner placed his finger on his notebook and peered at his writing. "The person was coming from the south. That's from the direction of the crime scene."

"That sounds promising," Scottie said.

"What time was that?" Gibson asked.

"Around nine forty-five."

"All right. Go on."

"Mrs. Lambert received a notice from the strata council about everybody keeping their doors secured. There had been a few burglaries in the area. So she didn't want to linger around outside. But she did have a good view of the person, if only for a moment."

Scottie had remained quiet until now. "Do you think she is a competent eyewitness?"

Gunner thought for a minute before he replied. "Yes, I believe so. She gave details. She said it was an adolescent boy, a teenager. He had long stringy hair. His clothes seemed unkempt. He wore a dark bomber jacket." He grinned once more. "She said he didn't appear to be a jogger. What do you think?"

"It sounds like we should go to the youth hostel. A lot of the street kids use it as a meet up. It's just across the park from the crime scene," Scottie said.

"Okay. Scottie can check that out later. The kid could be a witness."

"Or something more," Scottie said.

"Anything else?" Gibson asked, ignoring her comment. "What about anybody on the pier?"

"That didn't pan out," Na said.

Gibson provided a briefing of the post-mortem to the constables. There were so many things to undertake and a lack of personnel. He felt frustrated. It didn't help that his home life was a little crazy right now and promised to get crazier. Sometimes, he wondered if he could cope with all the changes.

"Go knock on some more doors. Widen your circle to the adjacent street," Gibson said. "And check for cameras. Both private and at the stores nearby."

"You bet," Na said and stood up. Gunner followed him out the door.

"Should we go to Kevin's workplace first?" Scottie asked.

She had been watching Gibson all morning. He was definitely distracted. She wanted to ask him what was troubling him, but she would find a better time to broach the subject. In the meantime, she thought it would be prudent to go along with him. He was the boss, so she didn't really have much choice. All she could do was follow orders and throw in her two cents' worth.

Chapter 10

"Do you want to grab a coffee on the way to the ferry?" Gibson asked. "I'm buying."

He realized there was some tension between them, but he wasn't totally sure why. Usually Scottie toed the line. Sure, she had her opinions on things, but this was something more. Almost a rebellion. Or was it all in his head?

"Sure. But real coffee, not the canteen crap."

"Okay. You decide on the place."

"And a scone."

They headed downstairs, out the door and across the street to the new bistro. It had opened last month for visitors from the cruise ships that docked there every day. It wasn't busy, so they got what they wanted and left.

"The ferry company's head office is closed on Saturdays, but I want to go to Kevin's actual workplace. We'll get the real scoop there," Gibson said.

"I agree." Scottie drove with one hand. Her other hand alternated between the steaming coffee and the warmed-up scone. She brushed the crumbs falling on her lap onto the floor.

The BC Ferry Corporation employed thousands of people throughout British Columbia. Swartz Bay was one of the major terminals, ferrying people from Vancouver Island to Vancouver and points onward on the mainland. The detectives had travelled by ferry many times but were unsure where to find the work sheds.

At the ticket booth they flashed their badges. The attendant directed them through the terminal and down a lane on the right. They drove through an iron gate and stopped in front of a large metal structure tucked behind a row of trees. Several trucks bearing the ferry logo were parked outside the garage. One door was open, showing a workshop with three hoists and five or six large standing toolboxes. The lone mechanic had his head stuck in an engine compartment, throwing a wrench around. At the sound of their footfall on the crushed rock, he stood up straight and rubbed his neck.

"Can I help you?" He scrutinized their appearance and added, "Officers."

"Is this where Kevin Meadows works?"

"Yeah, maybe." He leaned back over the motor and continued with his task.

"What does that mean?" Gibson asked.

"He works here, but not in this department."

"All right. Could you steer us in the right direction?"

"On the other side of the building. He works in maintenance. I think Ronny's there."

"Thanks."

The detectives tramped their way along a covered walkway. They came to a door clearly marked for employees only. Gibson grabbed the knob and pulled, but the entry was secured. He gave Scottie a disgruntled glare and banged hard on the metal surface. Nobody came, so he knocked on it harder. The staircase groaned under a pair of weighty footsteps pounding down the stairs. The door swung outwards. A paunchy, balding older man gawked at them. His coveralls were smeared with grease and dirt. Frayed shirt sleeves pushed back to his elbows looked like they had seen better days.

"What can I do for you?" A genuine grin spread across his ruddy face.

"Are you Ronny?"

"Sure am."

"We're searching for Kevin Meadows' workplace? Is this it?"

"Yes, it is. But he's not here today. He took some bereavement time. You know, because of what happened to his wife." His eyes twinkled. "But I guess you already know that because you're the police."

"Yes, that's right. Do you know if he was working on Thursday night?"

The man rubbed his chin in thought. "I'm not sure. Let's have a looky-loo at his timecard."

"Isn't there a schedule on a board somewhere?" Gibson asked.

"No. All employees log onto the company website to get their schedule."

Ronny walked back up the stairs with a heavy tread. The steps were weathered. The banister was worn smooth from umpteen palms that had run over it. The floor on the landing was scuffed and littered with dirt brought in from outside.

"Okay, let me see." The man stood in front of the time clock and picked out a card among the fifty or so in the metal slots. He plucked out a pair of glasses from his pocket and peered at the times marked in black ink. "Thursday. Kevin worked from 8pm to 6am. A ten-hour shift. That's about right." He handed the card to the detective.

Gibson handled the card, checking front and back. He took a picture of it with his cell phone. "What do these initials signify here?" He pointed to 'SBC'.

"That means the Spirit of British Columbia. It's the vessel Kevin would have been working on. Some of the guys do that."

"I see. Do you know who Kevin was working with?"

"Couldn't say. The cards don't have that kind of info." Ronny stared at the detectives. "You know we have quite a large crew working here on the night shift. We keep the ships in good order. There's lots to do. Safety and all that."

"Of course. I didn't mean to imply otherwise. Is there a supervisor we could talk to?" Gibson asked.

"No, he's on holidays. Kevin is the acting supervisor. Does that help you?" The man snorted. "But he still has to work his shift, not just sit on his ass like the regular guy does."

Gibson glanced at his partner.

"You could always go to head office and they could tell you everything you want to know. Schedules, partners, the whole kit and caboodle," Ronny said.

"Thanks for your help."

The detectives made their way out of the building to their vehicle.

"Well, I guess that lets Kevin off the hook," Scottie said.

"I don't think so."

"What? It's right there on his timecard."

"Really, Scottie. How naïve are you? That's an easy thing to fake, especially since he was the acting supervisor that week."

"I suppose."

"We need an actual person to verify that Kevin was at work all night. There's no security here. No guards. I didn't see any cameras. Kind of slack, if you ask me. He could have slipped away for a few hours if he had a strong enough motive to get rid of his wife."

"You have such a suspicious mind."

That's because I have my secrets. Gibson didn't say that out loud.

Chapter 11

The smell of smoke drifted in the window on the gentle ocean breeze. The scorched aroma could have come from a wildfire in the northerly regions of Vancouver Island. If the blaze was massive enough, the smoke could find its way from the mainland. It was late August. Typically, the fire season began earlier in the summer. But it had rained more than usual, keeping the forest floor damp.

Gibson stood in the living room facing away over the water with his coffee mug clutched in his hand. Beyond the upper side of the hills, a wispy haze blurred the blue of the sky. It had taken on a pinkish, orange glow. Gibson had hoped they would escape the miserable air quality this year. He was concerned about Katherine, in her condition. She would have to stay indoors and avoid inhaling the contaminants.

"I can smell the smoke."

Gibson turned around slowly.

Katherine's white nightie hugged her body showing her curves of softness. Her flowing brunette curls touched her slim shoulders.

"I better close all the windows."

"I'll brew some fresh Java. Are you sticking around at home today?" Katherine asked.

"I think I..." His cell phone pinged. He scanned the screen and read the text. "Perhaps not."

Katherine headed to the kitchen while Gibson made a call.

"What's up, Scottie?"

"My friend at the Royal Canadian Mounted Police heard about the murder and wants us to come by with a photo of the victim."

"Why's that?"

"He may have some information about her. If it's the same woman that came into his station a few weeks ago."

"All right. Pick me up." There goes my kayaking for the day, Gibson thought.

"On my way." Scottie hung up abruptly.

"Coffee's ready," Katherine shouted from the back.

"Be right there." He peeked into the newly painted room at the front of the house. No need for a baby reveal here—the powder blue walls said it all. Everything was in its place. The white crib was decorated with blue trim. Clothing and blankets in varying shades of blue were piled on a chest of drawers with the same embroidery. A rocking chair was tucked in the nook. Gibson moved down the hallway. He was dressed in a lightweight seersucker suit with a navy tie. From the lockbox, he grabbed his 40 calibre Smith & Wesson semi-automatic handgun. He clipped his badge onto his belt and headed to the kitchen.

"I'll take that coffee to go." He wrapped his arms around his wife and gathered her close. "That was Scottie. You need to stay inside. Promise?"

Katherine pursed her lip in a feigned pout.

"All right. I have a superb book to read." The kiss she placed on his lips was steeped in passion.

"That's unfair," Gibson said. He let go of her when a honk from a vehicle sounded in the lane. "My ride."

* * *

"Hey, did you get a photo of Dianne?" Gibson asked as he slipped into the passenger seat.

"Yup, I had one from the autopsy."

"Do you have any idea what this is about?"

"Not really, but Grant thought there may be a connection to our case."

Scottie drove into Sidney on the main street and struck a left on Fourth. They located the RCMP detachment in a grey building behind the Municipal Hall. The unit consisted of thirty-one officers, support staff, and a contingent of volunteers. Although its policing area was vast, its personnel were small-town friendly.

Constable Oscar Grant, Scottie's friend, greeted them in the lobby. He motioned them to a bench bolted to the wall. Scottie passed him the photograph.

"That's the lady. Dianne Meadows." He flicked the picture up and down on his hand. "Definitely."

"Don't keep us in suspense," Scottie said. "Spit it out."

"She came in about two weeks ago with some concerns. Her adolescent daughter" – he peered in his folder – "Virginia… At any rate, the mom discovered her daughter with this older boy. She thought he lived on the street by his general bedraggled appearance. You know the look I mean. Long, matted hair. Tattered jeans."

"How old?" Gibson asked.

"I say older because Virginia is only thirteen. Mrs. Meadows figured the lad was going on sixteen with one thing on his mind. Although she wasn't thrilled about that, what disturbed her more was the knife he had. Her daughter denied its existence, but Mrs. Meadows knew what she saw. She wanted to know if we could do something. Which we couldn't. She was bothered about the armed robberies around town and suspected the lad was involved. Mrs. Meadows was in a frightful state, I tell you. But what was I supposed to do with that? The kid hadn't threatened anyone. There's no crime in owning a knife. We would have to catch him with it concealed on his person, and then prove he had intent to harm someone." He shook his head, upset that he could have prevented the whole thing from happening.

"It's a coincidence. If the kid even had a knife." Gibson patted his arm. "And even if he did, we have no reason to believe that it's the same knife."

"I don't know. The whole thing gives me a bad feeling," the constable said.

"Can I see the file?" Scottie asked. She browsed through the slim report and said, "This could be our killer."

"What are you saying?" Gibson asked. "You're connecting dots that aren't even there."

"So what? Furthermore, Mrs. Lambert described the kid's clothing exactly the same as Dianne did. The jeans. The bomber jacket."

Gibson grabbed the folder from her hands.

"Street kids all dress the same."

"We should explore this lead. Now that we pretty well know that the kid had a knife. Maybe our supposed witness is really the killer."

"If they are even the same person. For Christ's sake, Scottie," Gibson said.

She gave him a hard stare.

"Fine. You were going to the hostel anyway. So why not check it out?" Gibson said.

Constable Grant sat back and crossed his arms. Their disagreement surprised him. As far as he was concerned, it was worth investigating further. That's why he had called her.

"Thanks, buddy," Scottie said to the constable and stood up to leave.

"No problem."

Chapter 12

The detectives headed to the parking lot. The smoke had flowed into the peninsula, reducing the brightness. Gibson gazed at the blood-red sun.

"So, I guess you were right about one thing," Scottie said.

"One thing? Thanks a lot."

"Perhaps Virginia was holding back. Let's go there now."

"Okay."

"And the bruises."

"Right." He turned to watch the poplar leaves quiver in the soft breeze.

Scottie traversed the back streets to the Meadows' house. All the drapes were shut. They mounted the steps and rang the bell. There was no answer. Gibson pressed on the bell longer the second time. He saw the living room curtain flutter, as if someone had taken a peek.

Virginia opened the door a crack. "My dad is sleeping." Her eyes were glacier blue and glassy.

"We want a word with him," Gibson said.

"I told you he's asleep. My mom just died, you moron."

The approaching footsteps had the clicking sound of leather-soled slippers. Kevin swung the door open wider. "Come in. I'll put on some coffee." His face was creased from lack of sleep, or worry. It was hard to tell which it was. The two-day stubble was ragged and grew in clumps on his jaw. He turned and headed toward the kitchen, his back hunched.

The murder had altered everything. The room had a bad smell. Plates with leftover food littered the counter. Unwashed teacups lay abandoned in the sink. Virginia plunked down at the end of the table. Sadness had drained the colour from her face. The detectives sat down and waited for Kevin to settle into a chair.

"We're sorry to bother you at a time like this, but we have several questions to ask," Gibson said.

"We don't know anything."

"Do you have a boyfriend, Virginia?" He turned to the girl.

"She's only thirteen," Kevin said.

Virginia played with the rings on her fingers, avoiding both her father and the detective.

"We understand there's a boy you hang out with sometimes. Isn't that true?" Gibson insisted. "Are you embarrassed because he lives on the street?" He held up his palm to restrain Kevin from interrupting.

"We're friends, Dad." Her eyelids fluttered.

Kevin held his tongue, rubbing at his mouth. His eyes glowered an angry black.

"His mom is mean." Her eyes darted around the room and landed on the dripping tap. The drops of water fell with a chaotic rhythm.

"Does he own a knife?"

"That's enough." Kevin pushed his chair back.

"It was for protection. From the crazies. He wouldn't hurt anybody," Virginia screamed in defiance.

"Your mother reported it to the police," Gibson said, leaning in closer.

"What the hell?" Kevin exclaimed.

Scottie stopped writing and looked up from her notebook. Gibson issued him with another warning to back away and carried on with his questioning.

Virginia fidgeted in her chair and pressed her hands together.

"What's his name?" Gibson spoke softly, attempting to cajole her into revealing all she knew.

"Ryder Simpson."

"Does he have a cell phone?"

"No."

"Where can we find him? At the youth hostel?"

She shrugged helplessly.

"Where do his parents live?"

"On Ardwell. His dad doesn't live there."

Virginia plucked her cell phone off the table and scrolled through to Ryder. She gave them an address. Her feet were bouncing up and down on the floor.

"Are you okay?"

"My mom and I had a fight." She blinked away the tears.

"What about?"

"Nothing."

Kevin looked as if he was going to lose it. He half-rose out of his seat, his hands on the table.

Gibson didn't expect he would get an answer, but he asked anyway. "Was it about the knife?"

Kevin blew up. "That's it. It's over." He jumped up, knocking his chair over in the quickness of his movement.

Virginia's eyes widened, terror slipped in behind them. Her mother had told her there was nothing to fear but fear itself, but her mom was dead. She started crying and ran out of the room.

"Virginia," Kevin yelled after her.

The front door slammed heavily.

"Well, that was uncalled for. You should leave her out of this business."

"Sit down, Kevin," Gibson said with some force. "We're investigating your wife's death, and we need some answers."

He sat, his rage smouldering.

"Your wife was pregnant. Did you know that?"

Kevin gnawed on his lip but didn't reply.

"How did Dianne get her bruises?" Gibson continued.

"What do you mean?" Kevin snapped. His eyes narrowed suspiciously.

"We saw marks on her body at the autopsy."

"She bruises easily. I don't know."

"Don't you?"

"No, I don't." He spat out the clipped words and shifted in his seat.

"What about the fractures?"

"She's accident-prone. I had nothing to do with that."

"Will the hospital records say that?"

"Why are you accusing me? Why don't you leave us alone?"

Gibson stole a glance at his partner.

"We'll talk again."

"We'll see about that."

"Thanks." The detectives got up to leave.

"Good riddance," Kevin hollered down the hallway.

* * *

Traditionally the suburbs were abuzz with people on the weekend, hanging out in the driveway, washing the car and chatting with the neighbours. Or out back, the kids would be running amuck through the sprinkler and playing lawn darts. But not today. The smoke was severely hindering all outdoor activities. If the wind blew any stronger, things could become worse.

Scottie drove down the desolate streets to the main road.

"I'm going to place a detail at Kevin's workplace. I want to find out if something funny is going on," Gibson said.

"What does that mean?"

"I want to see if he stays his whole shift."

"It's rather late don't you think? The deed is done."

"Yeah, I know. It's a gut feeling. It could be a habit of his, to just up and leave the workplace for a number of reasons."

"Like what?" Scottie asked.

"Lunch comes to mind. If it's easy to leave, it could have given him the idea to carry out his plan to kill his wife and still have an alibi," Gibson insisted. "Remember, he was the acting supervisor that night. That made it even easier for him to come and go as he pleased."

He crossed his arms as he fell back into his seat. That was a sign the conversation was over for now. He let his thoughts roam over the possibilities as he stared out the window. Could Kevin have been cheating on his wife and wanted to get rid of her? To move on to another life? Whatever the reason, Kevin was his prime suspect.

Scottie pulled off the highway and headed to Brentwood Bay.

"There you go. See you tomorrow." She stopped in front of his house.

The Sixties bungalow had a shake roof and weathered wood siding. Large fir trees towered over the backyard, but the westerly view at the front encompassed a tranquil bay with mountains in the background.

"Thanks." Gibson stood still and listened to the lapping of the water on the shoreline across the street. It was a sound he never tired of. He remembered about the letter again. The guilt felt like ice in his veins. He suffered guilt about everything in his life these days. Perhaps his position in the crime unit was too much for him. It was the first time he had harboured any misgivings about the job. He had a feeling Scottie saw it too.

Chapter 13

The following morning, Gibson sat in his office reading interviews and witness statements. The investigation was going in two directions, even though there were no solid leads. He set down the papers and leaned back in his chair. Although the floor-to-ceiling windows gave awesome views, Gibson stared at the ceiling. The team was meeting at nine for a briefing. The footsteps and chatter in the hallway announced their arrival.

"Have a seat everyone," Gibson said as they filed into the room.

Gunner and Na got comfortable in the chairs in front of his desk. As usual, Scottie opted to stand by the window. She stared across the Strait of Juan de Fuca to the Olympic Mountains of western Washington.

"The smoke is gone," she said and turned back to the room.

"How did the house-to-house canvassing go?" Gibson asked the constables.

"We didn't find any more witnesses," Na said.

"What about surveillance cameras? Any luck there?"

"The cameras at the waterfront condos point to the lobby doors, not out to the sidewalk."

"We do have the wine store on Beacon," Gunner said.

"Right. They have a camera aimed partly toward the street. But the film was too grainy to be of any help," Na said.

"Most of them were suits. No kids running down the sidewalk," Gunner added.

"That's it? No other cameras?" Gibson shook his head. "Fine, bring me the hospital records for Dianne. Was she admitted for domestic violence or was there a cover-up? Let's find out."

"Doctors don't do that," Scottie shot back.

"I want to see them," he said gruffly.

"How far back do you want us to go?" Na asked.

"Get it all."

Na shot a quick look at his partner. Gunner rolled his eyes.

"I also need surveillance at the ferry terminal."

"Huh?"

"Kevin works a late shift there. He'll be back on the job in a few days. I just want you to watch. Find out if he leaves at any stage," Gibson said.

"All right. Me and Gunner?"

"Yes. I know you have lots to do, but..."

"We're on it," Na said and popped out of his chair.

After the constables left, Scottie moved away from the window and sat at the desk. "They've got Kevin covered. Let's have a chat with Mrs. Simpson."

"Okay. Let's do it."

"I hope she's home." She flipped through her notebook. "Ardwell Road. It's not far from the Meadows' house."

They headed outside to a fine day. Scottie cruised down the highway, going northward. Gibson sat in the passenger seat with his legs stretched out. The conversation was stilted, so after a while they stopped talking. Scottie turned up the radio and kept her eyes on the road. The street they were searching for was closer to the town centre than she thought. There was a lot of construction going on. Nearly all the houses built after the war had been torn down. They were in varying phases of being supplanted by four-story condominiums.

Scottie pulled to the curb at a bungalow identical to several houses on the street. A small garden behind a white picket fence was well-tended with a riot of colour. A metal heron bird was nestled among a stand of cosmos flowers. They stepped up to the porch that was barely large enough for two people to stand on at the same time. Gibson knocked firmly on the door. A curly-haired woman with big brown eyes answered. She stopped short when she realized it wasn't her expected visitor.

"Can I help you?"

"Mrs. Paula Simpson?" Gibson held out his badge.

"Yes."

"May we have a word?"

"Is it about Ryder?"

"Yes."

"Did you find him?" She clasped her hands into fists. "Is he okay?"

"We're searching for him. May we come in?" Gibson asked.

"Of course." She opened the door wider and pointed to the right. "Will the living room do?"

"Thank you."

There was a dark sofa sprinkled with vibrant cushions like the garden outside. A remote control sat beside an empty mug and plate on the coffee table. Over the fireplace mantle, there was a modest TV with a picture on but no sound. One wall was covered with photographs of a young boy in different stages of his life. There were none of the father.

The detectives sat side by side on the sofa. Gibson bumped his shin on the table when he tried to cross his legs. Paula stood by the hearth.

"Is Ryder your only child?" He gestured to the photographs.

"What do you want with him anyway?" She tilted her head and eyed the detectives with suspicion.

"We're just asking questions. He may know something that could help us. That's all. We don't think that he has done anything wrong at this point, Mrs. Simpson." Gibson gave her a reassuring smile.

"Okay. I guess." She sank into an armchair. "I don't know where he is. I thought it was him at the door."

"He doesn't have a key?"

"When he doesn't lose it. Which is often enough." Paula blew out an exasperated sigh.

"How old is Ryder?"

"He's fifteen, and he belongs at home."

"Has he run away?" Gibson asked.

"That's one way of putting it. He'll be back though," Paula said.

"Would he be at his father's place or..."

"His father's dead."

"Sorry."

"What did you want to speak to him about? What could he possibly know that would help the police?" she asked, her suspicion aroused once again.

"Has Ryder been in trouble before?" He ignored her question.

"No." She looked up. "Okay. He has a juvenile record. It's nothing too serious. He stole something from the corner store. Ryder's a good kid. Not like his father." She clamped her hand over her mouth.

Gibson pulled out a card and passed it over. "If he comes home, give us a call."

"Sure." She put the card along the mantle. All she cared about was finding her boy, whatever he had done. "You'll call me if..."

"We'll stay in touch. Don't you worry." Gibson stood up. "Thank you for your time."

"I think she was lying about something," Scottie said after they had stepped outside.

"Maybe so. But more importantly, let's get a look at his juvenile record."

"Aren't they sealed records?"

"Sure. They are kept in a separate data bank so that the public can't access them. But we can."

"I'll get on that and do a thorough scrutiny," Scottie said. "Now we're getting somewhere."

Chapter 14

Gibson sat in the study and pulled out the letter. There were deep creases where he had folded and opened it a thousand times. He smoothed out the paper as flat as he could with his hands. The words were warm and touched on the emotional. A heaviness in his chest pressed against his ribs. He felt a sadness that made him feel alone. His eyes skimmed down to the signature again.

'Your son, Anatoe Sinclair.'

It took all his strength to pick up the phone. He stood on the brink of the swamp, willing it to swallow him whole. Gibson had no illusions about that. His past had caught up with him. He dialled the number.

"Hello."

"Anatoe?"

"Dad."

"I'm so sorry." Gibson placed the cell phone on the desk for a moment and wept. The darkness passed, and he picked it up again. The breathing down the line was even. "Are you here? In Victoria?" He choked.

"Yes. I would like to see you. Are you free now?"

"Meet me at the Brentwood Grill in an hour." Gibson hung up without waiting for a reply. His hands shook slightly.

* * *

Anatoe waited by the glass doors. His beefy square shoulders were pulled backwards, making him seem even taller than he was. He gave a crooked smile to the detective crossing the street. His earthy brown eyes sparkled in anticipation. Gibson made eye contact and picked up his tempo. His heart began to thump wildly in his chest. He halted in front of the stranger and bit down on his lip. Anatoe opened his arms. The warm hug felt right, like coming home.

They walked into the restaurant, father and son.

The patio was full, so they sat by the unlit fireplace inside. With drinks ordered, Gibson sat back in his chair and tried to act casual. They stared at each other, both uncertain where this was going.

"I found out about you this summer, when I was in Ontario. I wanted to tell you that I was your father, but…" Gibson ran his palm across his face. "How did you find out?"

"I got curious when you told me to say hi to my mom. So I asked her who you were." Anatoe toyed with the coaster on the table. His eyelids flickered. "She told me, but she wouldn't say why she kept it a secret from me. From everybody."

"Yeah, she kept it from me, too. We were both so young." Gibson blew out a long sigh. "I was stupid."

"I'm here now." Anatoe shrugged.

"How long are you staying in Victoria?"

"I've moved here." Anatoe held up his hand. "No need to worry, I won't..."

"That's wonderful," Gibson interrupted.

"Really?"

"Yes. Absolutely."

"I have plans."

"A garage like the one you had back east?"

"Kind of. You know about the Youth Justice Initiative Fund. Right?"

Gibson nodded. He knew they gave grants for the rehabilitation and reintegration of youth into the community.

"I applied for a grant and got funding for a three-year pilot project. I'm setting up a workshop and garage to teach mechanics to young offenders." Anatoe smiled. "I started out as a social worker, so I had a good chance to get the funding." Then Anatoe turned serious and said, "It will be a place for kids to hang out and learn at the same time. It's important to feel a part of something."

"That sounds great." Gibson grinned. His son had grown into a man of integrity.

Anatoe hesitated for a second before he said, "Don't take this wrong, but I know how it feels. I understand what these youngsters go through. They'll realize there's no bullshit with me."

"All those years." Gibson sighed again and hung his head. The scars were invisible, but the pain seeped out with his jagged voice.

Anatoe touched his hand. "Honestly. Focus on the here and now. That's all that matters."

Gibson nodded his head slightly. "What about your mom?"

"She thinks it's the right thing to do."

"Yes, she would."

"The funds are limited, and some expenses are ineligible. So I will have to contribute some capital, too. I'll probably do some fundraising through friends," Anatoe said.

"That alone will keep you busy."

"It will be crazy," Anatoe said and laughed.

The charged atmosphere settled into a cozy familiarity. They were comfortable together and talked the way best friends do—about everything, about nothing. The afternoon breezed by, a newly formed bond growing. The courage to trust others.

The light ebbed as the sun disappeared behind the crest of the hills. Gibson peered down at his watch and frowned. "Katherine should be home."

"Time to go." Anatoe downed the last of his drink.

They parted ways at the front entrance. Gibson walked toward the waterfront and without a backward glance skipped home.

Chapter 15

With a grin on his face, Gibson strolled along the street and around the corner to the narrow lane. Halfway down, he stopped at the bungalow. The fir trees that loomed over the house grabbed the final golden beams of daylight in its uppermost tips. The grounds were lost in the shadows that lengthened with the coming of twilight. A light at the end of the driveway flickered, and then flashed on. He stepped onto the porch and opened the door. Soft music and enticing smells drifted from the back.

"Katherine. It's me."

"In here." His wife shouted from the kitchen.

Gibson walked down the hallway and leaned against the door frame. Katherine's dark hair was pulled into a high ponytail. She was dressed casually in jeans and a green shirt with an apron tied around her waistline. Her chocolate brown eyes locked onto his smoky greys and ensnared his soul.

Gibson closed in to caress her face with the back of his hand. He swept his lips along the smooth curves of her neck and moved inward for a kiss.

"What have you been up to?" Katherine asked playfully as she kept him at arm's distance.

"It was a long day." Gibson sank into a chair. His anxiety showed in the way he plucked at his lips and gnawed inside his mouth.

"What's wrong?" Katherine sat in a chair opposite. Suddenly, her hand flew to the small of her back.

Gibson arched an eyebrow questioningly.

"It's nothing. A twinge." She pushed her hair away from her face. "But you?"

He was suffocating in his half-truths. No, his lies. Once he spoke there would be no turning back. He had to tell her about Anatoe. Or did he? If he didn't, and it slipped out one day that he was the father, then...? It had happened long ago. Long before they had even met. But that wasn't the problem. The pickle was he had kept it from her. And then, the other thing. What happened in Ontario was just last month. Would his marriage survive his betrayal? He could keep that part to himself.

Katherine stared at her husband, watching his eyes flicker. His hands clasped and unclasped.

"Just tell me the part that I actually need to know."

"I went to The Grill today. To meet someone."

Katherine sat completely still.

"Anatoe. From Ontario." With a sigh, the tension in his neck loosened up. It was just a first step. A faint uplift of her lips gave him the resolve to carry on. "Anatoe Sinclair. He's my son."

Katherine's face washed blank with bewilderment. The rosy colour drained away until only a paleness was left. Her neck muscles, soft and willing only moments before, tensed into a stringy mass. Her shoulders sagged a little.

"This isn't your first." She put a hand on her belly.

"I'm sorry. I didn't know about Anatoe until this summer."

Her hand met his for a second, smooth and tender.

"We're okay."

They talked late into the night, all cuddled under the blankets. His wife had always found it hard to forgive herself for her failures, but she possessed the power to forgive others unequivocally. For the first time, Katherine was content with her lot. She had a real crack at being happy. Without any preamble, she opened up about her fears of motherhood, and at the same time, the excitement of a new life. She prattled on about baby showers, pushing a buggy down the lane on crisp early spring days and watching her child fall asleep in his crib.

Gibson felt relief that he didn't have to drag up the past. Things he did, or worse, should have done. He was supposed to be the strong one, but when he looked at Katherine, he realized he was the weak one. He had taken the easy road. Now he felt as if he stood still, unable to find his direction while everyone around him was moving forward. He had so many doubts. Gibson pushed that away and shared Anatoe's dreams and aspirations with her. He talked about the program for young boys that Anatoe was going to be a part of. And how much he had accomplished already. There was pride in his voice when he spoke.

"You're a good father."

Gibson grimaced and pressed her hand.

"I know people that may be able to help with funding," she said. "In particular, there is a man I met while volunteering at the community centre in Sidney. I'll call him later. Jackson."

Gibson's ears pricked up at the name. "Parker?"

Katherine turned back to face him. "You know him?"

"Yes." Gibson said. "But not in good circumstances."

"Oh."

"It was the loans manager at his branch who was murdered."

"Oh, my God." Katherine shook her head.

"You leave that stuff to me." He lifted her chin and gave her a slow kiss. "Are you feeling sleepy?"

She giggled and pulled the cover up tight.

Chapter 16

It was a really good morning. Gibson hadn't gotten a great deal of rest, but he felt freer after unburdening his bottled-up secrets. Well, some of them, at least. It was enough to put a spring in his step. He bounded up the stairs to his office, leaving the elevator for the undisciplined people. It wasn't until he plopped himself down in his chair that he noticed he wasn't alone. Scottie was standing by the window and had turned to face him when he entered the room. The expression on her face spelled trouble. The folder by her side told Gibson it was big trouble.

"What is it?" He moaned. There was enough to do as it was. The pressure in his head started to build into a headache almost immediately.

"There was another stabbing." Scottie moved over to the empty chair in front of his desk and flopped the file on top. "It took place late last night. After the pubs had closed."

"Was it fatal?"

"The young girl is in intensive care. A Carol Barton."

"Okay." He hoped the girl would be all right.

Scottie flipped open the file. There were only a couple of pages. "It's being handled as a robbery at this level. So it's not ours."

"That's good," he said.

"Unless she dies. Then it's ours."

Gibson folded his arms and frowned.

"Do you think they're connected?"

"I have no idea." Gibson shrugged. "I hope we get the forensics soon. Are you..." His cell rang. "Just a sec." He peeped at the screen and answered, "Gibson." After a few shakes and grunts, he hung up. "That was Na. The hospital won't give us Dianne's medical files without a warrant, but they will let me speak to the doctor there. Apparently, she went to a few different doctors. That in itself seems suspicious."

"Guess that will keep you busy today," Scottie said.

"What about you?"

"I was going to hit the hostel. Try to track down Ryder."

"Okay."

Scottie got up and started to leave. "We're on the same team, Gibson."

"I know." He listened to her footsteps as she headed down the stairs. With his finger ready on the speed dial button, he got another call. "Gibson." It was Na again.

"I got a heads up from a lady in HR at the ferry corporation. Kevin will be back at work tomorrow."

"All right. Are you and Gunner set to take that night shift and watch the guy?"

"You bet," Na said.

"Good. What about the timetable for the maintenance crew?"

"She said we would have to call the crewing scheduler for that."

"Get on it." Gibson hung up.

Chapter 17

There were several hospitals in the area. Gibson had guessed that the one out on the peninsula would most likely be where Dianne would go for treatment. It was the closest to her house. Na had called two other hospitals further afield, in case she had been trying to hide her injuries from the authorities—there had been so many incidents. But luckily for them, Dianne never thought that far ahead. Maybe she should have thought about getting help. Mind you, Gibson was assuming domestic violence was involved. With these thoughts occupying his mind, he failed to stop at a yellow light and was confronted with the blare of a horn. He sped up and flew down the highway.

The Saanich Peninsula Hospital was a squat building spread out in every direction except up. At the front desk, he inquired about the administration area. The cheerful, plump lady who greeted him pulled a map from a pile beside her right arm and with a Sharpie drew a line that wiggled across the paper, end to end. She marked his destination with a star.

"Just follow the line." She looked behind him to the next person.

Gibson turned toward the first hallway and with his head down as he walked, he managed to bump into several people scurrying down the corridors before reaching the administration office across the aisle from the dispensary.

"Hello. I'm Detective Gibson." He yanked out his badge and flipped it open. "Dr. Hawthorn is expecting me."

"One moment, please." She pushed a button and muttered a few words before she hung up.

"Take a seat. He's on his way." She pointed to a bench along the far wall.

"Thank you." Before Gibson could sit, a doctor with a well-fitted suit and brogue shoes approached him.

"Hello. I'm Dr. Hawthorn. This way."

His office was two doors down. A polished nickel plate with the doctor's name and rank was screwed on the side of the frame. Gibson almost laughed at the absurdity of it all. So typical of government facilities—many layers to get to the top dog. And this man was the top dog. He had so many initials after his name, it made Gibson's eyes blur. The doctor gestured to the leather sofa beside a window that overlooked lush gardens.

Dr. Hawthorn sat in an armchair and faced his guest. "How may I help you, detective?"

"We're looking into the injuries of Mrs. Meadows. We want to know if she was a victim of domestic abuse."

Gibson waited, but nothing was forthcoming.

"The pathologist found bruising and several poorly healed broken bones. They hold no bearing on the attack that claimed her life."

"I see." The doctor moved around and folded his hands into his lap. "Even so, I am not at liberty to hand over any medical files without a warrant. But I have read over everything we have on Mrs. Meadows and I'm prepared to discuss these with you. Will that do?"

"Yes. It would help steer us in the right direction."

"Do you think this is a domestic violence case?" the doctor asked.

"Yes, I do." He locked eyes with the man.

"I was afraid of that." He tapped the folder with the pencil he had been spinning in his fingers. "I must say that I agree with you. Unfortunately, Mrs. Meadows saw numerous doctors over the years. Our turnover of staff is quite high, and all the reports were paper not digital like they are now." He broke off and lowered his gaze. "I'm not making excuses, but I had to gather this lot from several different areas of the hospital." He tapped the folder again.

"Then the police were never involved?"

"No. We failed her."

Gibson got up and shook the doctor's hand. "Thank you for your time."

He left the room, turned the map about and found his way backwards to the main entrance. With a wave of his hand, he thanked the lady at the front and headed to his truck. He sat quietly, trying to think who it was he had been planning to ring earlier in the day. And then it came to him, the baby shower. He dialled the number he had been given by Chelsea, but nobody answered so he left a message. Before he could start his vehicle, his cell rang.

"Gibson."

"This is Linda Miller. Is this the detective?"

"Yes. I just tried calling you."

"Sorry. I heard the phone ring as I was unlocking the door." Her voice was low and husky. "Is it about Dianne? I heard what happened. It's terrible."

"Yes. Were you and Dianne friends?"

"Not what I would call a close friend or anything. I met her at the bank when I was getting a loan last year. We got along nicely and would go for a coffee and chat occasionally. I didn't know her well, but I liked her."

"Okay. Could you tell me what time she left the baby shower?"

"Oh, dear. Dianne never made it to the party."

"I see," Gibson said. "Did she phone to cancel?"

"No. She just didn't come. By nine o'clock, everyone was leaving. I was going to call her the next day to see if she was okay, and then I heard..." She faltered, a quick intake of air finishing her sentence.

"No problem. Thank you for your help."

"I wish I could have helped." Linda let out a sob before she hung up.

Gibson wasn't sure what he thought about that. Where had Dianne gone that evening if she hadn't gone to the shower? There were several hours unaccounted for. And why had she lied to her husband as to her whereabouts? Was it just an excuse to get away from Kevin? From the beatings? It was beginning to look like he was on the right track.

Chapter 18

It didn't feel like Gibson was on the same team. He said yin, when she said yang. There was absolutely no evidence to suggest that Kevin was the killer. He had an alibi. She couldn't see any motive. Maybe Kevin had beaten his wife, but that didn't always lead to murder. And sure, the spouse was always a possibility, but the weapon of choice was normally a gun.

Gibson was wasting their meagre resources on a fishing expedition. What was the thing about staking out Kevin's workplace? Scottie didn't want to kick up too much fuss, but really, that was a stupid idea. Especially because there was too much to do and not enough bodies. Although the police chief said it was on the books to increase personnel, nothing materialized from his promises. And so, with her mission in hand, she stomped down the pavement to the hostel, determined to find Ryder.

The old clapboard structure had stood on the same spot for forty years. In spite of the storms that blew in from the southeast, spraying saltwater into the air, the building was presentable with a fresh coat of paint. All the windows had bars inserted into the frame. Not to keep people in, but to keep thieves out. There was an expanse of grass with large borders of shrubbery between the hostel and the skateboard park. Lots of places to hide and attack innocent pedestrians. An invitation to take what wasn't yours.

Scottie tugged on the front door and entered a narrow, dimly lit hallway. On the right, a young boy with an earring looped through his nose sat on a stool reading a magazine. At the sound of footsteps, he lifted his head and gave a once over to the intruder.

"No women allowed in the hostel."

Scottie pulled out her badge and flipped it open inches from his nose ring. "I have a hall pass."

"Take a pisser. I don't work here." He glowered at her and took hold of the magazine from the counter as he stormed out the doorway.

A stout middle-aged man swaggered into the reception area from a back room. It was apparent that neither his age nor his build would be a disadvantage when force was needed to curtail unruly behaviour. He was a tough looking bugger. Maybe a bouncer in another life. He greeted Scottie.

"What can I do for you, officer?"

"I take it you're in charge." Scottie flipped her badge anyway.

"Tom."

"Is Ryder Simpson here?" she asked, assuming this would be his hangout.

"I haven't seen him since last week."

"Are there any bodies in the bunk area right now?" She pointed down the hall.

"No. They're out on the streets doing their hustle, I suppose."

"There was a boy at the counter when I got here. He took off."

"That's a new kid," Tom said. "Just got off the bus from Toronto. He wouldn't know Ryder."

"Who works here?"

"There's four of us in all. Stud only does the nighttime shift." The corner of his lip twitched with a held back smirk.

Scottie narrowed her eyes.

"Oh, hell. He has so many studs through his nose, his lips, his eyebrows, and..." Tom shrugged. "What else could we call him?"

"I see." Scottie wanted to say call him by his real name, but it was probably something inane like Mickey.

Tom picked up the phone. "I'll make a few inquiries. Hang on."

When he was on his second call, a young girl came in and sauntered past them to the rear. No girls, eh punk, Scottie thought.

Tom hung up and cried out, "Hey, Cherie."

Was that the girl's name or was he calling her darling? Scottie was really growing impatient. In the end, only Stud had anything to say. He had seen Ryder on Thursday night. Around midnight or so. He had scurried out quickly, even after Stud had called out to him. Yeah, he thought it was a bit weird, but he had only seen the kid at the hostel a few times.

"I had things to do. Ryder wasn't staying, and it was time to lock up for the night," Stud said over the speaker phone. "I can't remember what he was wearing. You're kidding me, right?"

"Thanks, Stud," Scottie said.

Tom hung up the phone. "That's the best I can do."

She left her card on the counter. "In case Ryder comes back. Give me a call anytime. I don't care what time it is, just make sure he doesn't know you're calling me."

Scottie left the building feeling deflated because she wasn't sure where to hunt for Ryder. Tom had given her a few places to check out. At the last moment, he had riffled through the folders in a steel cabinet and handed her a photo that had been taken upon Ryder's arrival at the hostel. She was thankful for that, but unfortunately his head was lowered and a cap was pulled over his eyes. It would be hard to recognize Ryder from the image. Like Gibson said, they all looked the same. She needed his sealed records, and she needed them now. There was sure to be a proper photograph of Ryder in the documents. Scottie pulled her cell phone out to call about the file. Her finger wavered over the screen. Who else could she call?

The RCMP Investigative Data Bank could only be accessed one way—through the Canadian Police Information Centre (CPIC). And, they had made it clear: 'Don't call us, we'll call you'. Scottie didn't want to piss them off. She pocketed the phone and hopped into her vehicle. Time to take to the streets and see what she could round up the old-fashioned way.

Scottie cruised the back streets to the highway, did a U-turn and headed back toward the waterfront. Most of the street was one-way, so she did the loop a couple of times, taking it slow so she could search each side. There was a street musician with a guitar case at his feet, open for tossed coins. And with any luck, a few notes. A black and white mixed breed dog lay quietly by his side, its head resting on its paws.

Scottie stopped her vehicle and hopped out.

"Do you know this guy?" She showed him the mediocre photo of Ryder.

"No, I don't think so." The musician squinted at the picture. "Try the mall at the top of the street. Lots of kids use that as their meet-up spot."

"Thanks." She tossed a coin into his hat and left.

On the third time round the block, Scottie spotted a group of teenagers hanging out in a shopping centre parking lot. She pulled over to the curb on the opposite side and slowly made her way over, as if she was headed for the coffee shop. There were lots of people in and out of the stores, so they didn't pay her any mind until she was on top of them.

"Whoa there, big boy." She stepped in front of an oversized kid, blocking his line of escape, and flashed her badge for the hundredth time that day. "You're not going anywhere."

"I didn't do anything." He puffed up his chest and snarled.

Scottie placed her hand on her gun and raised an eyebrow. Not a threat, just a reminder of who was in charge. The boy's body went limp with his arms dangling by his side, his bravado rebuked.

"Whatever," he stated in a meek voice, not willing to give in to authority completely.

"I'm looking for someone." Scottie put her hands back on her hip.

"We don't know anything," a squirt of a boy said. He moved in close to his buddy and gave him a jab—a warning to keep his mouth shut. With a flick of his wrist, his smoke hit the side of a BMW. He narrowed his eyes at the detective. "You got a problem with that?"

Scottie swallowed her smart remark and shoved a photo of Ryder in his face. "Does this guy look familiar to you?"

"I don't know, man."

"Ryder Simpson. Does that ring any bells?"

A shrug of the shoulder and a contemptuous pfft noise was all she received in response.

"Have you seen him around?" She figured they knew who Ryder was. It was a small town with one main drag and one hostel.

The four boys snickered and turned to walk away. The squirt tugged on the fat boy's sleeve to get him moving.

"I have cash."

They kept on walking.

Ah, shit. Scottie went back to her vehicle and sat for a few minutes, scanning through her email messages. Her cell had been vibrating in her pocket throughout the hostile encounter. A rap on the window startled her. The squirt had his face plastered against the glass and mouthed, "Open up."

She quickly unlocked the door. The kid hopped in and sank into the seat, so his friends wouldn't see him cavorting with the enemy.

"Move it."

Scottie squeezed into the long line of traffic.

"You got a name?" She was met with silence.

"How much is it worth to you?" the squirt eventually asked.

"Depends on what you got?"

"I know where Ryder is."

"How do you know him?"

"We got into a fight. He had this knife," he said. "He threatened me. No one threatens me."

"Okay. Twenty bucks."

The squirt tilted his head and laughed. "You can do better than that."

"I have about twenty-eight dollars on me. It's all yours." Scottie kept her eyes on the road. Her jaw felt stiff from holding back on what she really wanted to do. She wanted to give the kid a shake.

"All right. He's camping at Horth Hill Park."

"There's no camping allowed there."

"Duh. He's in hiding, lady." The kid rolled his eyes and put out his hand.

Scottie turned down a side street and pulled over. She delved into her wallet and hauled out her cash.

The squirt jumped out of the truck without even a thank you.

Chapter 19

Scottie cruised back to the promenade. The squirt was probably headed to his dealer. The remainder of his gang from earlier were nowhere to be seen. No street kids at all, not even the musician in front of the liquor store. She made a left onto the main road and headed back to Victoria, trying to decide her next move.

Horth Hill was a large park. It wasn't as if she could saunter up the first trail and find Ryder hanging around a tree, chit-chatting to some teenage girl. Or sitting on a log and having a smoke. No. Not by a long shot. He would trek off the beaten path and find a small gully where he could hunker down and avoid being picked up. His movements since the murder made her sure that he knew they were coming for him. Otherwise, why would he leave the hostel at midnight?

Scottie needed to put a team together. But how could she convince Gibson of the importance of doing this? A ping from her cell phone broke her reverie. She peeped down to a text from her partner. It was a good thing he had written the message in all caps, otherwise she would have had to pull over to read it. 'URGENT MEETING. ASAP. AHOD'. That meant all hands on deck. Did this mean there was a shift in the investigation? Scottie flipped the switch for her flashing lights and vanished down the road as quickly as she could.

Scottie made it to the station within thirty minutes. She hurried into the building and up the stairs two at a time. With a slight break to take hold of her breath, she came to a stop on the threshold. Gibson turned from the window when she came into the room. Gunner was ensconced in a comfy chair, idly flipping through a muscle car magazine. Na sat quietly in front of the desk, reading through his notes. Both gave her a wave.

"What's going on?" Scottie asked as she flopped into the last vacant chair.

"Jocko called for us to get down to the lab."

"What has he got? Why didn't he tell you on the phone?"

Gibson held his hand up. "Hang on. I'm getting to it." He walked over to his desk and sat down. "The results were mixed. Jocko wants us to see for ourselves. So that's what we're going to do."

"Good, let's go." Scottie jumped up quickly.

"One other thing."

She sat back down with a thud. Gibson handed her a small envelope. "The sealed records were delivered ten minutes ago."

"And?"

"Not a great deal. Ryder got probation and some community service for theft under $5,000. It was a shoplifting charge. He stole some stuff at the corner store by his mom's place. Just like Paula said. They were easy on him because it was a first offense as a minor. No violence or weapons were involved."

"Still."

Gibson passed the arrest photos, front and side shots, to the detectives. Ryder appeared extremely young. By the expression on their faces, everyone thought the same.

"He was fourteen at the time. There is a father listed on the intake papers. With an address."

"So Paula lied. He's not dead."

"It seems so. Or maybe he died after the incident." Gibson shrugged. "In any case, the important thing is we have Ryder's prints."

"Goody. Goody." Scottie rubbed her hands together.

The forensics laboratory was on the main floor. They shot down the marble staircase, four pairs of boots making a racket. Gibson opened the door to a room cooler than the rest of the building with a buzzing sound from the electronics in the air. Although Jocko kept the place spotless, it was overcrowded with equipment, glass beakers, Bunsen burners, and more.

The forensic lab technician sat on a stool, reading through a report. His rumpled clothing hung off his lean form. Standing up made him appear even more dishevelled with the trouser cuffs at his heels skimming the floor.

"Okay, everyone's here. Let's get started."

He clasped his hands together as if in prayer and scooted over to a counter at the back of the room. The team followed and stood around in a semi-circle beside him.

"There was plenty of blood on the knife." Jocko gave a warning not to interrupt, his eyebrows furling into one line. He would go at his own pace. "And as a bonus, I also found traces of blood under the hilt of the knife. It was a very small amount but enough material for DNA comparison."

He picked up the knife in its evidence bag, turned it in his hand and passed it to Gibson.

"I got the results from the National DNA Data Bank this morning. The blood on the blade was from the victim. So, this is the murder weapon." Jocko paused to break the bad news. "The traces from under the hilt are an unknown."

"Damn it," Scottie said. "But it will be the killer's blood, right?"

"No comment." Jocko only dealt in concrete facts. He left the theories to the detectives. "When you get a suspect, I will be able to tell you more by comparing the samples."

Gibson nodded his head slowly, satisfied there was promise.

Jocko moved along the counter to another apparatus.

"This was one of the trickiest jobs I've had to do in quite some time," Jocko started. "Latent prints on non-porous material tend to be fragile, so they must be preserved as quickly as possible. But I didn't get the knife until the following day..." He drew in a deep breath – not an excuse but disappointment. "It was a challenge, but I did get some results. Maybe not exactly what you wanted. I used a Cyanoacrylate fuming technique. That's super glue to the layman." Jocko laughed. "This procedure was the best chance I had to get any prints at all." He waved his hand back and forth at his audience. "Never mind, that part doesn't matter to you."

"Did you get a hit?"

Jocko stared at Scottie and continued. "I found one good print that I ran through AFIS (Automated Fingerprint Identification System). There were no strikes. The other print was smudged. I got a partial from it, although its quality was poor. Sorry, but I couldn't run that one through the system. It simply wasn't clear enough. But I would be able to compare it, if I had a print to compare it with. That was a mouthful."

"We have Ryder." Scottie held up the print card from the juvie arrest.

Jocko took the card and laid it on the counter. He studied it for a moment, tracing the lines with a pointer. "There are a few..."

"Is it him?" Scottie asked.

Jocko ignored her and continued searching the suspect print. He opened a drawer and pulled out a magnifying glass. "I can't find ten points of comparison here. Don't worry. Let me run his prints through AFIS. It'll only take a moment."

They stood around quietly. There was no small talk, just restless movements and a shuffling of feet until the computer spat out the answer. Jocko held up the slip of paper. His eyes twinkled.

"Ryder Simpson. It's a match to the print on the knife."

"I knew it." Scottie snorted and jabbed her partner on the arm.

Chapter 20

"I think I know where Ryder might be hiding out," Scottie said.

All eyes turned to her in disbelief.

"Why didn't you say so?" Gibson asked.

"I just did." She stuck out her tongue.

"Cough it up."

"The word on the street is he's camped out in Horth Hill Park."

"Where's that? Never heard of it," Gunner said.

"It's in North Saanich. Across the highway."

"Is it like a grassy field and a pond and ducks and stuff?"

"No. What part of hill didn't you get?" Scottie asked.

"Oh, shit. You mean we have to hike up a mountain?"

"Enough everybody," Gibson shouted over the mêlée. "How confident are you about this?"

"Well, I had to bribe a kid, but I think it's worth it. We have nothing else."

"I don't know," Gibson hesitated. "Let's head back to my office and think this through. How do we know the kid wasn't lying?"

"Yeah, I know. It's not much to go on. I suppose my idea is kind of lame." Scottie shrugged. At the time, she was stoked to go and hunt Ryder down at the park. Now, she was totally unsure about it.

The detectives marched back up to the second level. They had just sat down and began a discussion on whether to do a search of the park when a growl on the stairs distracted them from their game plan. The police chief popped his head around the corner.

"Don't you guys have a home to go to?" Rex asked. He looked around for somewhere sit.

"Take my chair." Na jumped up.

"That's all right. I'm not sticking around here too long. It's been a tiring, stressful day. What's going on?"

"We have a possible suspect hiding out at Horth Hill," Gibson said. "We don't have any real intel, so it could be a big waste of time. And I don't think we have enough resources to do a good job anyway." He didn't mean to be so blunt, but he was growing tired of constantly having to make do. It wasn't a good way to run a major crime unit.

Rex let that remark go by. The lines on Gibson's face showed the nervous tension he was feeling. "How many people do you need?"

"Five. Maybe six," Gibson said.

"I'll get some constables from the local RCMP to join the hunt. When is this happening?"

Gibson checked his watch. It was rather late into the afternoon. He realized there were only three hours of daylight left. There wasn't any time to make a real plan. They would be going in blind and hit as many trails as they could. "How about one hour in the park's parking lot?"

"Done," Rex said and left the room. He shouted down the hallway. "Good luck."

"Thanks. We'll do our best."

"I'm ready." Scottie stood up again.

"Not yet. We need to bring a few provisions together first. Flashlights, walkie-talkies." Gibson tapped the desk with a pencil. "How many walkie-talkies have we got? Are they charged up?"

"There's at least a dozen of them in the supply room. They should be fully charged," Na said and headed to the door. "I'll get those together. And the flashlights."

"Everybody meet in the garage," Gibson shouted down the hallway. "What else? Do we have a map of the park?"

"There's one at the entrance," Scottie said.

"That will have to do. Let's grab some water from the cafeteria."

"All right. Should we take the Suburban? It's the roomiest."

They darted down the stairs, anxious to start moving.

* * *

By the time the team arrived at the park, they had lost an hour of daylight. The volunteer troops were stationed in the parking lot as Rex had promised. Five hefty men and one woman dressed wisely for combing the forest. They seemed more prepared than his people. At least Na had changed into a pair of jeans, and they all had on solid boots. The search unit huddled, shoulder to shoulder, around an aluminum map screwed to a post beside a bulletin board. It marked the major trails, but probably not to scale. Better something than nothing at all! There were five ways into the park. With ten people, that would make five teams of two. So far so good, Gibson thought. A pair of eyes on each side of the trail.

"Thanks to everyone for coming out. Our suspect is unlikely to be armed, but be prepared, in case. I don't want anyone getting shot. Remember, he's a kid."

"Do we stay on the path, sir?" An officer addressed Gibson.

"Ryder will not be on the path. He will have chosen a route through the undergrowth to find a hiding place. So search for evidence of that."

"Understood."

"Should we call for backup upon sighting the subject or move right in?" The woman officer asked.

Gibson studied her height and heavy frame and held back a smirk. "I believe two people can overcome him." He was thinking she could do it on her own.

"Any more questions? Check your radios. Make sure we're totally on the same frequency."

There was a bit of shuffling and rearranging before the squad set off. Gibson chose the centre trail with Na. Scottie and Gunner took the vertical track to the summit. With a steady pace, Gibson trudged along the soft path. Twigs and leaves crackled under his boots. He kept moving forward as the incline steepened, his heart thudding loudly. The silence of the forest was not absolute. Birdsong came in lulls and surges. The birds fluttered around in the boughs and over his head. The canopy was dense, allowing little sunlight to reach the forest floor. Even the undergrowth was choked with brambles and thick shrubs. Gibson stumbled on an exposed tree root, his legs feeling heavier the higher he climbed.

Up ahead, the light seemed brighter. He stopped in a clearing, squinted at Na and took a swig of water. They shook their heads, acknowledging nothing of interest yet and walked on, the woods once again enveloping them into its darkness. A rustle put them on alert. They stood frozen, trying not to make a sound. A debris of stones tumbled down the slope, accompanied by heavy steps and a thump. The detectives readied themselves for an encounter with the suspect, crouching down in the bushes, but instead a deer crashed through the brambles, bounced over the track and vanished into the brushwood. As they waited motionless, ears sharper, the hush of the forest returned. The brightness was fading quickly, so they picked up their pace, even as the path ahead faded into the gloom, and their nerves stood on end.

* * *

It had taken Ryder only a few weeks to get used to the sounds of danger. He sensed them now. The forest had its own language, an uneven motion of wildlife and trees. What he heard today was the steady rustle of humans, creeping up on him.

Only once had he been taken off guard by another runaway. Since then he had learned how to listen. That boy had crept up on him as he slept, tucked beneath bleachers at the school, a safe overnight spot. Apparently not so safe. The boy had jumped him and almost got away with it. Ryder had hit him so severely, it even surprised himself. That was when he bought the knife. The very next morning he strolled into the hardware shop on the upper side of the main street and doled out his hard-earned cash for a little security. But Ryder was defenceless now. His knife thrown away in a panic.

He dropped his sandwich and slipped from his camp.

* * *

The forest seemed ominously quiet as Scottie and Gunner stood in the improvised camp. Which way had Ryder fled?

The radio crackled and stopped Gibson and Gunner in their tracks.

"We found his hidey-hole," Scottie whispered. "We're near the summit. There's a half-eaten sandwich, so he's on the run. He could be coming down fast."

"Is he coming toward us?" Gibson asked.

"I don't have a lead on his direction. Remain vigilant."

Scottie peered into the shadows, unaware that Ryder stood only a few metres away. The snap of a twig made her turn, just in time to see a white flash from the corner of her eye. She ran toward the clumsy footfalls as her prey scrambled noisily through the brush.

Suddenly the chase was on.

The radio crackled once more, and then a call rang out up ahead.

"Police. Stop." That was Scottie.

Gibson and Na ran toward the sound, raspy breathing slowing their progress as the path narrowed to a sharp incline. The radio crackled and hissed.

"Everyone stay in position," Scottie said, as she accelerated her pace to a full run.

Gibson knew she wouldn't even be breaking a sweat yet. The beating of her boots resonated down the hill, but grew fainter as the echo was swallowed up by the woods. Gibson could hear the beating of his heart as he pushed onward.

* * *

Scottie ran as fast as her legs would permit, leaving Gunner in the dust. Broken sprigs whipped across her face as she crashed through the undergrowth. Thorny bushes clawed at her and entangled her clothing. A spiky branch snatched her jacket, and she stumbled to a halt. She fought to pull herself loose, ripping her jacket in a desperate move to get up. As she barreled through the forest, her bare arms took the brunt of the slices and gashes from the unforgiving scrub. She felt her lungs screaming for air, and her heart thumping as hard as she had ever felt. Every once in a while, she would detect him, and then Ryder would vanish from sight. She knew she was losing ground; she could no longer perceive him thrashing as he rushed to get away. The gap was getting more substantial.

Somewhere in the distance an owl hooted—the first sound of the nocturnal animals waking up. A rabbit bolted across the way. She stopped to listen and saw a deer path barely visible in the darkening light. It would cut through to an upper route, but would it be in the right direction?

* * *

Ryder ran through the undergrowth. He was small and quick and flew under the branches and spines that would tug and tear at everything that made contact. This forest was his friend. He had explored its paths and ways as a kid. The shout to stop made him sprint faster. He heard the yells of the others and let his fear drive him forward. His heart beat frantically, and his breath came in small spurts as he shot out of sight. He knew their guns and other gear would weigh them down. But once in a while, the lady appeared close behind. His worn runners slowed him down, so he crunched lower to pick up speed. Soon he felt her presence fade into the background. He walked slower, breaking once in a while to take heed. The sounds were in the distance.

* * *

Scottie jostled her way along the narrow trail and popped out at the crest of a ridge. She heard the crunch of something undefined. She turned toward the sound. Ryder stepped out from the shadows, just ten metres away. They locked eyes. Ryder jumped off the ledge and tumbled away.

Scottie hesitated for only a moment and followed him over the cliff. She landed on her back with a hard thud. The snap vibrated up her leg and thundered in her ears.

In the intense silence, the scream made Gibson's blood turn cold.

Ryder paused, but just for a second. Then he disappeared.

Chapter 21

"He escaped." Gibson didn't have the energy to explain any further.

"You mean to tell me that one small boy got the better of ten police officers?" Rex shouted down the phone.

Was there a question in there or was he rubbing it in? The police chief certainly wasn't impressed with the outcome of the search. Gibson sank back into his chair, wishing he had broken something and was sitting in the hospital at this very moment. He supposed he had better tell Rex about that. Only the chief wasn't finished with berating him. Gibson tapped the pencil against the desk in frustration, waiting for a lull in the conversation, so he could tell him the really bad news.

Gunner stuck his head round the door. Gibson wasn't in the mood for a chitchat and scowled at him, just as he had done with Na ten minutes earlier. The constable didn't need any more convincing to move away. Gibson turned his attention back to the phone. There were things to settle with the police chief first.

"Does Scottie have any other ideas where Ryder might hide out now?" Rex asked. "Seeing as he probably won't go back to the park."

That was a dig that Gibson didn't need or want. He drew in a breath and let it out slowly before speaking.

"Scottie's in the hospital. She fell and broke her leg. They operated early this morning." He pulled the phone away from his ear anticipating the roar that came down the line.

"What the hell? What are you guys doing?" Rex yelled. "You better get your shit together, Gibson." He hung up.

"She'll be all right," Gibson said to the hum of the broken connection.

All right, then. That went smoothly enough. He lowered his head to his chest and rubbed his temple. Now might be a good time to find the father. Maybe that's where Ryder would flee to next. He couldn't think of the guy's name. Scottie had the folder somewhere. He got up and walked down the hallway to her office.

Early morning light filtered through the leaves and cast a greenish tinge in the room. The envelope was lying on the desk where she had flung it the day before. Gibson sat in her chair and pulled the file out. He flipped through the pages until he found the name. 'Guy'. It seemed like a misprint, only he recognized it was a French name. Gibson hoped the man hadn't moved back to Quebec. He stared out the window, trying to figure out how to locate this man. The eastern view toward downtown was nice—very different from his waterfront vista.

He rubbed at his overworked thigh muscles. His body was as tired and sore as his mind was. He couldn't think of the last time he had gone for a hike. Uphill at that. He wondered how the others were doing. They were a good deal younger than him. He needed to start exercising more. The thought of that made him even more achy. Gibson wandered back to his office and popped a couple of pain relievers. The search party had been a major failure, especially since Scottie had been hurt. He put his hands behind his head and closed his eyes. The rest of his team would be in soon.

"Are you all right, boss?" The fresh smell of coffee floated into the room. Gunner held up a big cup. "Latte for you. The way you like it."

Gibson motioned him to sit down. "Thanks." He took a sip.

From the hallway, the elevator creaked as it ground to a halt. Na stepped into the room and plunked into a chair. His eyes were red as if he hadn't slept in a week. Gibson imagined they were all pretty tired out from last night's chase.

"Let's move on from yesterday," Gibson said.

The constables nodded in agreement.

"Did you have any luck with the crew scheduler from the ferries?"

"The guy was very co-operative. I was totally surprised. Being a big company and all," Na said.

"What did he give you?"

"We got the employee schedule for the maintenance department at the terminal." He pulled out several pages from an envelope and handed them to Gibson. "This is the timetable for the whole month."

Someone, probably Na, had highlighted Kevin's name, making it easy to see his schedule.

"Last Thursday he worked with George Wright."

"Did you get this guy's contact number?"

"You bet."

"Good. What did he have to say?"

"I didn't get a hold of him yet. There was no answer."

"Okay." Gibson ran his finger down the page. "George won't be working again until tomorrow night. Looks like he's paired with Kevin again."

"What do you want us to do?" Gunner asked.

"Let's stick to the plan. Surveillance tonight. If nothing comes of it, go back on Thursday night," Gibson said. "When that shift is over have a chat with George regardless of whatever else happens. How does that sound?"

"That's great," Gunner said.

"Go home and get some rest this afternoon. It'll be a long night for you guys."

"Thanks." Na struggled to push himself up from the chair.

"Those are some wobbly legs."

"Not used to hiking."

"We're all in the same boat."

The DCs headed out.

Gibson sat back in his seat. He could feel the pills taking hold. After a few moments, he leaned forward and punched Guy Simpson into the database.

He got a hit. "Well, well. What have we here?" Gibson picked up the telephone and dialled Scottie's friend at the RCMP. It took several minutes to reach Constable Grant's desk.

"Grant." His husky voice had a friendly ring to it.

"Hey. It's Gibson. What can you tell me about Guy Simpson?"

The constable laughed. "What's he done now?"

"Nothing that I know of. It's Ryder's dad. The boy with the knife."

"Right. I've had a few run-ins with him. Robbery. Never gives up. I saw his name somewhere lately."

"He was just released from Wilkinson jail a month ago," Gibson said.

"Hang on a sec. We get bulletins when any local jailbirds are back in the community. That's probably where I saw his name."

Gibson heard a drawer slam and some rustling of papers.

"There's no address. He's not on parole," Grant said. "So he has no obligation to tell us anything."

"That's a bummer."

"Why did you want to know?"

"I was thinking Ryder might go to his dad's place to hide," Gibson said.

"Sorry. I wasn't any help at all. Call any time."

"Thanks." Gibson hung up and put an 'x' through that task. There was no way to find out where Guy landed up after being released. He could even be on the streets. At least he understood why Paula had denied his existence. He was a real loser. She had sound grounds to fear for her son's welfare with that bad influence. Not somebody to look up to for guidance. Gibson had to admit it wasn't looking good for Ryder.

Chapter 22

It felt weird without Scottie hanging around. Even though they had their different way of looking at cases, more so lately, he missed her yang. It was almost time to visit her in the hospital, so he stuffed Ryder's file back into the envelope. One of the pages slid off the desk. He stretched over to pluck it up and moaned. "Shit." Every muscle in his body had seized up. He felt like somebody had handed him a righteous beating. The only thing lacking was the purple welts.

He remembered Dianne's bruised and battered body. How did that all fit in? It seemed logical, at least to him, that Kevin was the murderer. Only it was Ryder's prints on the knife. Was there another explanation for that? There had to be more. Gibson's mind flitted back and forth. He popped a couple more pills and stood up. Scottie's office was darker now that the sun had moved around the building. Gibson flipped on a light and placed the envelope back where he had found it.

As he turned to go, he stumbled and bumped the side of the desk. The monitor screen lit up and cast an eerie glow across the room. He was surprised Scottie hadn't shut her computer down. It wasn't like her to just up and leave. But he supposed everybody had been in a such a rush yesterday, it had been forgotten. He reached over to turn it off and observed the display. There was a video in frozen mode. Gibson pulled out the chair and sat down. It was the surveillance from the wine shop. The film was as grainy as Na had said. Gibson guessed Scottie must have been reviewing the film for herself. He regarded the date and time stamp. It read: 9.29 pm Thursday. She had already watched the whole thing. Gibson shut it down and popped the USB memory stick into his pocket before he left Scottie's office.

* * *

The hospital was more than halfway to Sidney. Gibson cruised down the road feeling dispirited by last night's round of events. As long as Scottie recovered completely, he wouldn't have a problem putting it behind him. He turned left off the highway, and then right at the entrance.

The receptionist flashed her teeth and directed him down the centre aisle. Scottie's lodging was to the right, then a left, second door on the right. Gibson hesitated and strolled into the room with a light step. There was barely enough space for the single bed his partner was slumped in. The dozen or more flower arrangements took up the rest of the space, their scent failing to overpower the chemical smell. At the sight of a friendly face, Scottie made an effort to sit up.

"Hey. Don't bother." He gestured around the room. "Lots of admirers." He plunged into the lone chair, feeling stupid – he had forgotten to get her something.

Scottie leaned back onto a stack of fluffy pillows. She seemed uncomfortable with her leg in a sling, held high in the air. Her face was pale with two dots of pink on her cheeks. A tube ran from a bag of liquid to a needle stuck in her arm. The beeping from a machine beside her sounded steady, reassuring.

"That's one hell of a contraption," Gibson said. "You getting along okay?"

"I guess." Her voice was softer than usual. Probably from the drugs she was taking.

"When are you getting out?"

"Four days, maybe. Many weeks of walking with crutches." Scottie shuddered. "Did you hear my scream?"

"Yes."

"It hurts as much as it sounded." She grimaced. "He got away. Damn it all. I tried."

"You went above and beyond." He almost tapped her cast, then thought better of it. "We don't know where he went."

"Ryder didn't have his bomber jacket on. Just a white shirt. Maybe it was a tee shirt."

"We didn't find his jacket anywhere around the camp site," Gibson said. "Wonder where he ditched it?"

"Hmm. What did Rex say?"

"I think you know."

"I suppose I do."

"We'll find him." It was an empty promise, but it made her smile.

"Yeah. Sure." Scottie closed her eyes.

"I'll let you rest now. I'll come back later."

"Gunner was here earlier."

"That's nice."

"He told me the girl that was stabbed is in a room a few doors down on the right. She's going to be okay."

"That's good." Gibson had read the report from the first officer at the scene. Apparently, the girl was dragged into an alley and stabbed three times. The attack had been brutal, and she had been badly injured.

"Yeah, poor girl," Scottie agreed. "Pass me that water, would you?"

After she had a long sip, Gibson put the plastic cup back on the tray. He turned to say something else, but she had fallen asleep.

"Sweet dreams."

Gibson left the room and walked down the hallway to find the girl. At the third door he saw her name in a placard fixed on its surface. 'Carol Barton'. She was a slip of a girl, almost lost in the folds of the cotton bedding that covered her from tip to toe. She looked up when Gibson rapped on the door frame.

"Hello. Are you a doctor?"

"No. I'm a detective."

"Have you found who did this to my daughter?" A tall lady standing by the window turned toward Gibson.

"No. I'm not on the case. Just checking in to see if Carol is doing okay."

"She's doing well. I'm taking her home tomorrow," Mrs. Barton said.

"Good." Gibson lingered in the doorway.

"He was just a kid." Carol's eyes were wide and filled with tears.

"I'm sure the police will get him," Gibson said and turned to leave. Like he told her, it wasn't his case. He could always ask the officer in charge if they had any suspects. Like Ryder.

"He had a tattoo on his wrist. A symbol or cross."

"You take care now."

He walked down the hall and peeked into Scottie's room. She was still out like a light. As he plodded back to his vehicle, his legs protested. He found some aspirin in the console and swallowed a few. He knew who the girl's assailant wasn't. No tattoos on Ryder.

Chapter 23

A drive to the office seemed almost insurmountable at this point, what with the rush hour in full swing. It would have been easy to take off for the rest of the day. With Scottie in the infirmary and the DCs resting up for their stakeout, who would complain? But Gibson wasn't that kind of person.

Furthermore, there was the tension he was feeling about his plans for the evening. He had suggested inviting Anatoe for dinner and Katherine had agreed. It surprised him she hadn't been haranguing him about it. The approach of motherhood was having a calming force on her moods. Even when faced with the revelation that Gibson had a son, it didn't seem to bother her. He hoped this state of tranquility would prevail over the coming months. Besides, he thought it prudent to stay away from the preparations his wife would be making at home and get back to work. As a consequence, he sat in a long line of vehicles leading to town. As if on cue, his cell phone rang. He viewed the screen.

"Hello."

"When are you coming home?" Her voice was quietly untroubled.

"Ah. In a few hours." He was uncertain if this was the calm before the storm or whether she had come to terms with the situation.

"Pick up some wine. I'm making jambalaya."

"White, then?"

"That would be nice. A Gewürztraminer?"

"Okay. See you soon." Katherine blew him a kiss and hung up.

The traffic was practically at a standstill. He moved slowly in a stop-start fashion. As he rounded a bend in the road, he saw a blue light flashing up ahead. An accident. That explained the gridlock. There was a car rolled over onto its hood in the ditch. A truck faced the wrong way and blocked one lane. Gibson inched slowly forward. As soon as he passed by the scene, the highway opened up. He flew the remainder of the way into the city.

* * *

Gibson sat in his office, his feet propped up on his desk. They couldn't decide anything more about Ryder until he showed up someplace. But he had other things to check out. He still considered Kevin a likely suspect. Gibson perused the phone records of the Meadows family. They revealed nothing unusual. Calling each other, keeping tabs on the kid. No clandestine meetings with lovers from either of them. Although he was sure Kevin was having an affair. He pushed through some paperwork so it wouldn't bog him down. There was always too much red tape. Read this. Sign that.

He placed his hands behind his head and leaned back further into his chair. He was still puzzling over why Dianne had been at the pier. Why did she lie about going to the baby shower? Could it be she was meeting someone? Was that someone the father of her unborn child? Did Kevin ambush them? Were they both having affairs? So, which way was it? It was all conjecture and stabs in the dark. He lacked any facts.

Gibson lowered his feet to the floor and stood up. Not only was this case complicated, but thoughts of the evening ahead added to his muddled mind. It was simply too much. He gave up and headed home.

* * *

The aroma of spices filled the house. Gibson peeked into the dining room to see how things were going. Katherine had pulled out all the stops to make a favourable impression. She had dusted off the fine china, a wedding present from a steadfast friend. The silverware gleamed from a recent polish. A pair of candle holders flanked a large crystal vase in the centre of the table. The V-shaped container overflowed with pink roses and snow-white flowers Gibson didn't recognize until a sweet scent, reminiscent of strawberries, floated up to his nostrils. Freesia. He poked his head into the kitchen and watched Katherine stir a simmering pot on the stovetop. With a flick of her fingers, she added a pinch of Cajun heat. She turned at the sound of his inhale.

"You like?"

"Very much." Gibson grazed her cheek with his lips. "I'll get changed. Anatoe will be here soon."

Did he catch a flutter of uncertainty in her eyes? The sensation had come and died so fast he wasn't certain.

* * *

Anatoe arrived with a bouquet of daisies, a bottle of expensive wine, and a twinkle in his eyes that reminded Gibson of his son's mother. He had constructed scenarios in his mind of how the evening would go. Not all of them were good. The introductions had been awkward. Had his negative emotions brought it on? Instantly he felt his pulse throbbing in his temple. The two people he cared about the most stood motionless for longer than Gibson could handle. He sputtered some words of welcome and steered them into the living room. Almost as soon as Katherine sat, she sprung up from her chair.

"I have to check the food." She fled to the back.

Gibson directed an uneasy glance after his wife. Anatoe didn't seem to notice. "Let's sit at the table. I'll get the wine." Gibson wanted to get the night over with quickly. Eat and run. Why had he supposed this was such a brilliant idea?

They both sank into their chairs. Gibson sat at the head of the table and Anatoe took a place beside him, capturing the view to the backyard. They chatted amicably, the alcohol smoothing the raw edges of Gibson's nerves. Katherine entered with a big platter of steaming food and put it on a trivet. She sat opposite Anatoe and forced a weak grin.

"Enjoy." The word defied her expression.

"Is everything okay?" Gibson asked. "Are you feeling all right?"

"I'm fine. I just want everything to be perfect."

"It is. The food, you, my dad," Anatoe said. He pressed his lips together, unable to say all that he felt. His chin trembled like a child, grateful for the love.

Katherine smiled warmly.

Gibson wished he wouldn't always imagine things would go badly.

Time rolled by pleasantly as they exchanged stories. Most came from Anatoe. His upbringing. His passions. He had started out as a social worker. But his interest in cars had steered him in a different direction. And now, with the realization that he wanted to be part of something bigger, something meaningful, he had embarked on a novel venture. From the beginning, the support of his mother had encouraged him to walk the straight and narrow. He knew how fortunate he had been. Ryder hadn't been so lucky.

Katherine sat forward in her chair, drawn into Anatoe's enthusiasm. She promised to entice community leaders to support him. Jackson Parker from the bank was already on board.

As the hours passed by, nobody wanted the evening to end. Even the occasional silence was comfortable. But end it must. At the door, Anatoe reached out and hugged Katherine in a gesture of fondness and admiration.

Gibson stood there quietly. He wanted to remain lost in the moment a while longer. But the details of the case seeped back into his thoughts unwanted. People were afraid to go out at night, and the papers were spreading rumours that the town was sinking into chaos. Not unlike how Gibson was feeling. One minute, bobbing on top of the waves, and the next, falling away into the darkness. The more he doubted himself, the more troubled he felt. The separation between his personal life and his work had blurred. It was the second time he thought he should quit.

Chapter 24

Gibson couldn't shake the gloomy feeling, not even on this bright summer day. A noise from the hallway made him turn from the window. The DCs lumbered into the room and sat down. Their clothes were wrinkled. Gunner had a coffee stain on the front of his shirt.

"Long night, boys?" Gibson returned to his desk and propped his feet on a lower drawer he had pulled out earlier. He waited with expectation for good news.

"Long and not productive," Na said.

The inspector groaned. They needed a break in the case. Although Gibson figured surveillance at Kevin's workplace was a waste of time, he wasn't ready to give up. Well, not yet anyway. Gibson sensed that there was still something missing.

"One more night?"

"Okay. No problem."

"Don't forget to visit Scottie in the hospital before you head home. She would appreciate some company," Gibson said. "Give her an update on what's happening."

"Is there anything happening?" Gunner asked. His mischievous grin bordered on mocking.

Gibson shook his head. He guessed Gunner would always have that little boy mentality. Most of the time he kept it under wraps. They were stressed by any lack of progress. Same as he was.

"We're going there directly," Na said. He yanked at his partner's jacket. "Come on."

The DCs walked out and went down the stairs, yapping about this and that. Gibson could hear their boisterous chatter until they rounded the corner. Then silence reigned once more. He sat at his desk, weighing his options. With his mind made up, he strolled to the laboratory to have a natter with Jocko. After some discussion, he left the station with an envelope tucked under his arm.

Gibson reckoned Kevin was one of those guys who might stop at the pub for a couple of drinks before heading home. But he thought he would take his chances and drive into Sidney with intentions of confronting him. Seeing the murder weapon might shock Kevin into opening up, even confessing. It would be a bonus if Virginia was there. She had more answers to his questions than she was letting on, he was sure. He pulled up to the house and stopped. No light shone through the drawn drapes. He knocked once on the door and waited.

A bleary-eyed Kevin answered. With barely a glance toward the detective, he turned and walked away. Gibson accompanied him down the hall to the kitchen. Virginia was slumped in a chair messing with her hair. A half-eaten slice of toast lay abandoned on the plate in front of her.

"What?" She rolled her eyes when he sat down opposite her.

Kevin poured himself a cup of coffee and leaned against the counter. "What can we do for you? Did you find the killer?" He snorted, an ugly sneer pulled a lip down at the corner.

Gibson remained silent, pulling the glossy photos out of the envelope and placing them on the table.

Virginia squeaked.

Kevin stared at the array of pictures. "What the hell do you think you're doing?" His gaze met the detective's hard steely stare. "That's not mine."

"But you know whose it is. Don't you, Virginia?" He waited for a response, but she turned her head away.

"Is this the knife Ryder had?" he demanded once more. As far as Gibson was concerned, there was only one answer. After all, Ryder's prints were on the handle and it would be too weird for there to be more than one knife. Would she tell him the truth?

"Do I have to say?" She glanced over to her father.

"I think that would be a good idea at this point. You don't want to be involved with this punk's mess. Jesus Christ." Kevin flopped into a chair and sighed.

Virginia reached over to a close-up shot and pointed to a mark on the handle. "Right there. Ryder scratched two 'x's, so he could prove it was his. You know. In case someone stole it."

"Did somebody steal it?"

"Not exactly."

"Well?"

"We were making out on the couch." She fidgeted and gawked at her father. "I suppose the knife fell out of his pack somehow. Actually, my mother found it. We fought." Tears welled up in her eyes.

Gibson held up his hand when Kevin started to speak. He suspected there was more to the story.

"Mom put it in the shed. After she died, and you came here..." She swallowed hard. "I looked. It was gone."

"Did Ryder return to fetch it?"

"I don't think so..." She paused. "No. How would he know it was here?"

"You didn't tell him?"

She shook her head slowly.

"What about you?" Gibson turned to Kevin. "Did you find the weapon and kill your wife?"

"Piss off." He leaped out of his chair and pointed a shaky finger at him. "Get out!"

Virginia ran from the room.

Gibson let himself out and hopped in his truck. Why hadn't Dianne turned the knife into the cop shop? Maybe because the police hadn't helped her the first time she went in with her concerns. So the question was, if Ryder hadn't taken the knife, and he saw no reason why Dianne would have taken it with her to the pier, who did that leave? The husband. And that's who he thought was the most likely suspect. Only he couldn't arrest Kevin on a hunch or a premonition. It was like asking a psychic to find a missing person. There was nothing he could do without evidence. He was completely stymied.

With so many contradicting ideas clouding his thoughts, he drove around aimlessly. The town had undergone a tree beautification period twenty years earlier. Now trees stretched down each street, making dapples of light and shadow on the pavement. Gibson ran into a dead-end street lined with a row of shimmering grey-silvery poplars. He retraced his steps and turned at the next corner onto a familiar street. An older model car was parked in the driveway of a bungalow. The plethora of flowers out front waved in the air. He drew alongside the curb, walked through the small gate and rapped on the doorway. It was a few minutes before it was answered by Ryder's mom, her curly hair now a mass of tangles. Paula stood with a hand holding onto the neck of her quilted housecoat. She stuck her head outside and swept her eyes down the street as if Ryder would be there.

"You're alone." There was a rawness to her voice as if she had been up all night crying.

Gibson nodded slightly.

"Come in. I'll make us a fresh pot."

Paula shuffled down the hallway in her floppy slippers. The detective closed the door and followed. The air in the kitchen was thick with the tang of burnt java. She switched off the coffee maker and poured out the dregs from the bottom of the carafe. Her movements were robotic, indifferent to the day. After fussing with the mugs and cutlery, she sat across from Gibson.

"The murder weapon has Ryder's prints on it."

Paula gasped softly.

"It was his knife," he said.

"He didn't do it."

"I don't think so either." Gibson was surprised at himself. As soon as he said it, he realized he didn't think Ryder had anything to do with Dianne's death. He was putting himself in a precarious position, but he didn't give a shit.

"Really?" A slight twitch played at the corner of her mouth, revealing her fear. Gibson could see by the longing in her eyes that she wanted to believe him. But she possessed an inherent mistrust of the police. "You're the only one that thinks that."

"Have you heard from Ryder?"

Paula shook her head sadly.

"We really need to get him to come in. Just to talk to him." Gibson paused. "Will you tell me the truth?"

"About what?"

"About Ryder's father, Guy Simpson. I think Ryder might have run to him for help."

"He wouldn't go to Guy for anything."

"Why's that?"

"Guy is his stepfather. They never got along."

"I see."

"So, I guess now you're going to ask me about his real dad?" Her eyes flared with anger. "Well. I'll tell you anyway. I was raped so that's a dead end. Isn't it?" She sucked in a lungful of air and puffed it out. "Now you know everything." She burst into tears. The drops ran down her cheeks and dripped off her chin. Her body heaved, broken by short pauses of recovering breaths. Before long, she was still.

"It's okay."

"No. It's not. It's my fault Ryder went off. He overheard the conversation between me and his stepfather. Ryder wasn't meant to know about the rape." Paula was on the brink of crying.

Gibson pressed her fingers.

"Will you help us?" she pleaded.

"I'll do my best."

He had an idea. Maybe it would become a plan. He would keep it to himself for now.

After Gibson left Paula's house, he felt wretched. He hoped he hadn't promised too much, predicting a bright future that may not be there. He could be fooling himself. Scottie could very well be right. Everything pointed to Ryder at this point.

Chapter 25

The mountains in the distance were silhouetted against the baby blue sky. A flock of geese crossed low over the misty water. The birds were on the move to southern climes. Gibson stood in the front window and watched the first arbutus leaves drift down to the ground. Signs of the changing season were all around. The air smelt of the ocean, the salty sensation tickling his nostrils.

He polished off the remainder of his espresso and headed back to the kitchen. Katherine was still asleep, so he forewent breakfast. He didn't want to wake her just yet. She was resting for two. There was always the café across the street from his office. Gibson closed the front door quietly and hopped into his truck. He drove down the highway, sorting his plans for the day. Scottie was still in the hospital and on his list for a visit. He had to call Na to see how things went at last night's surveillance. It was probably nothing, another dead end.

He pulled into a space on Dallas Road and walked along the pavement to the coffee shop. After a full breakfast and a latte, Gibson strolled across the street. He fumbled with his card key to unlock the door to the building. The office was dark, so he flipped on a light.

When he picked up the paperwork stacked on his desk, he moaned. Someone at the administrative centre had been busy. Then a thought popped into his mind. This was a job for Scottie. He smirked at the prospect of passing the buck. She wouldn't be fully mobile for weeks and weeks, but she would be back in the office, broken leg or not, very soon. There wasn't anything that would stop Scottie from pushing on. His phone pinged. He glimpsed at the screen and flopped into his chair.

"Gibson."

"It's Rex." His rich baritone voice rumbled down the line. "Have you found that kid yet?"

"We have several leads we're chasing," he lied.

"All right. How's Scottie?"

"She's getting along fine."

"What's Gunner working on?" Rex asked.

"He's on a stakeout. With Na." Gibson stifled a laugh. Rex was constantly asking about his nephew.

"Good work. Keep me posted."

"Always," Gibson said.

The police chief hung up.

Gibson stared at the folders and sorted through them. It really was the very least he could do. Some were bulletins needing an initial, proving he had read them. Not the type of proof the courts needed, that was for certain. There were way too many to peruse, so he signed them all. After several hours, he tipped backwards in his chair and stretched his cramped muscles. The office had been quiet all morning, so the hammering of feet on the stairs seemed thunderous. If he had to guess, it would be Gunner and Na with some good news.

The constables hurried down the hallway and stood in the doorway. Na was wheezing heavily.

"You're out of shape, old man." Gunner laughed.

"So, what's the scoop? Anything?"

"Yeah. Kevin left the terminal halfway through his shift."

"Really?" Gibson leaned forward. "Where did he go? Did you follow him?"

"Hang on, boss. He walked to the docks at Canoe Cove and got on a boat."

"It was a yacht called *Sea You Later*, down on Dock G," Na said. "It was immense. Megabucks." He rubbed his thumb and fingers together to emphasize his point.

"How long did he stay?"

"Two hours. We think he was playing poker."

"There was a great deal of whooping going on," Na added.

"Did you talk to George, Kevin's workmate?"

"No. We stuck with Kevin. By the time we returned to the workshop, George was nowhere to be found," Na said.

Gibson sat back in his chair and mulled over what the constables had found. But he wasn't sure how this news would help his case. He let his thoughts lead him forward. If Kevin had left the terminal to play poker and nobody noticed his absence, then it was conceivable that he could drive into Sidney, kill his wife and be back before anyone was the wiser. Yes. That fit into his theory. He would go to Canoe Cove and find the owner of the boat and ask the tough questions. Was there a game last Thursday? Was Kevin there? And what about George? It wouldn't take long to wrap this up. He was closing in.

"When is George scheduled to work again?" Gibson asked.

"Sunday."

"Ah, shit. Have you got a number for him?"

Na flipped through his notebook and gave his boss the info. Gibson also took the name and berth number of the yacht.

"Great job, you guys. Catch you Monday unless something comes up."

"Thanks. I have a soccer game to get to," Gunner said and flexed his arms.

After they left, Gibson gathered the stack of files he had compiled for his partner. He walked down the hallway to her office and placed them on the desk. After checking his watch, he realized visiting hours at the hospital had started. He stepped outside to a warm day. The sun had burned off the last of the mist and dispelled the dreariness. When he arrived at the hospital, it surprised him the parking lot was empty. He strolled into the lobby and greeted the receptionist. She threw a little half-wave his way.

Scottie was sitting on the edge of the bed with her broken leg stuck out in front. The white plaster was covered in signatures. She scratched at the itchy skin inside the lip of the cast with a plastic fork.

"How are you doing?" Gibson asked.

"I'll be fine. Back to work before you know it."

It was just as Gibson thought.

"Any news about anything?" Scottie asked, stifling a yawn.

"It's slow going. But Na and Gunner saw Kevin leave the ferry terminal a few hours into his shift."

"Really? Where did he go?"

"To the marina. Maybe playing poker. So, I wasn't off the mark about how easy it was for Kevin to disappear for a while without anybody taking notice," Gibson said.

"I feel so useless sitting here."

"Get some rest. I'll see you later. I have things to do," Gibson said. He looked back as he left the room. Scottie had leaned back into a pillow and closed her eyes.

Gibson sat in his truck and pulled out his cell phone. It was the second call he had made to George. There was no answer and no voice mail to leave a message. He chose the main road north, passing Sidney on the way to Canoe Cove. The last turn before the terminal veered right. He turned onto a narrow roadway that led to the docks. There was a sign that showed a pub down a dirt lane. A stand of trees hid it from sight. He had heard it served good food and beer on tap. It would be the perfect spot for a belated luncheon.

Another twenty metres along, the road opened up to the harbour. A big parking lot with numbered stalls ran next to the water, separated by a low railing. He found a spot marked for visitors and stepped out onto a rutted tarmac. The smell of bottom paint and barnacles assaulted his nostrils. It was a working marina. He could hear the sound of power tools and the screeching of gulls high above. The scarred wooden docks creaked as the swell rocked against the pilings.

Gibson fumbled with his notebook to recall the name of the boat and the berth number. He strolled to the end and found Dock G. Aluminum boathouses crowded near the ramp, housing the most expensive yachts. A brisk breeze had kicked up, causing the dock to jar with an erratic movement. Even with his experience on the ocean, it was difficult to walk a true course. The boats tugged on their moorings as the wind strengthened. A rogue wave crashed full-on and sent a spray of saltwater into the air.

'Sea You Later'. Gibson stopped in front of a twenty-metre yacht. He peeked at his notebook once more. This was it then. He moved toward the stern of the boat and knocked on the hull. Someone shouted at him, but he couldn't understand what they were saying. He just waited.

A young girl came out of the cabin. The mop in her hand dripped a soapy liquid on the deck. "Can I help you?"

"I'm looking for the owner." Gibson flashed his badge so he would get some response.

"Sorry, I'm the hired help. Mr. Hopkins isn't here."

"Do you..."

"I don't know anything else," she interrupted and shrugged. "I guess you could ask at the office."

"What can I do for you?" The shout rent the air.

Startled, Gibson stumbled forward. He reached out and managed to grab a stanchion, saving himself from tumbling into the brink.

"Sorry, didn't intend to frighten you."

The detective turned around to face a giant of a man with loose jowls and thinning hair. His eyes flashed with a friendly spark. His smile was wide and genuine.

"Are you Mr. Hopkins?"

"No, I'm his buddy," he said. "Hopkins will be back the day after tomorrow."

"Were you on the boat last Thursday?" Gibson asked. He released his hold of the metal rod and got back his sea legs.

"Oh, I see. The poker game." He chuckled. "Are we in trouble for having a wee bit of fun?"

"I don't care about the game. Only who was there that night."

"Hopkins was on board last week. Certainly not me. So I don't know who else was there on that particular night."

"Have you got a number for Hopkins?"

"Won't do you any good. He's somewhere up the coast on a friend's sailboat. I believe they were headed to Desolation Sound. The cell service that far north is almost non-existent. But they should be docked around noon. Their slip is over there." He pointed across the water to the next float.

"Could you tell him I need to speak to him?" Gibson gave him a card.

"Sure thing."

Gibson walked back to his truck and drove to the pub. He ordered a beer and slumped in his seat, fuming. Sunday was two days off. He thought he had it in the bag, but he was no closer to pinning down what Kevin had been up to last Thursday. He wanted to wrap this up quickly. The gods had other plans for him.

Chapter 26

It was a waiting game. Waiting for forensics, for alibis to be broken, or evidence to appear.

Gibson wound up his lunch and drove into Sidney. He parked by the pier and took a walk along the path. A park bench tucked behind some tall ornamental grasses was a good spot to sit and watch the waves roll in. The rhythmic motion of the water was soothing. Across the strait, a narrow slip of sand stretched past the northern tip of an island. A flashing signal at the end marked the danger. Farther in the distance, the majestic peak of Mt. Baker glistened in the sun.

Gibson leaned back in his seat to think. He needed to find out more about the victim to figure out the killer's motive. Kevin wasn't saying much. He wouldn't be telling them he had a girlfriend and wanted to get rid of his wife so he could start a new family. But Gibson thought that's exactly what had happened. Who would know about a girl on the side? His family, neighbours, co-workers? A fellow like Kevin might brag about his affair at work. That was a definite possibility. Only, Kevin's co-workers were not very forthcoming. He should go back and crack some heads. Someone must know something. George might know. Gibson dialled his number. Again, he didn't get an answer. Did the guy have call display? Was he avoiding the detective because he knew the truth?

Gibson phoned the BC Ferry Corporation. His call bounced from one directory to another. He punched repeatedly on the 'O' key, hoping to get connected to an individual. All he heard was 'Sorry that is an incorrect entry.' He stopped trying to beat the system and listened to the options—select one if... a real person answered. He asked for Liz in Human Resources. Na had given him the name. Five minutes later the lady was on the line and gave him the address he sought.

"All right, George," Gibson mumbled to himself. He strode back to the truck and headed across the highway to North Saanich. The country roads were narrow and tree-lined. He took a lane that ran toward the west side of the peninsula. Several signs warned of deer crossing. He slowed down and remained vigilant to any movement in the shrubbery off the shoulder. Number two-thirty-two was perched on the hillside. He rode up the paved drive and ended in front of a two-story home with an attached garage. The curtains were all drawn. It seemed like nobody was home.

Gibson walked up the steps of the veranda and rang the bell. He could hear it echoing throughout the house. While he waited, he peeked in a window by the doorway. It was tough to see inside, but he didn't believe anyone was hiding in there. He pressed the buzzer once more. After a few moments, he gave up and strolled to his truck. He looked up at the first-floor windows, but all was still—no fluttering of curtains or moving shadows.

Gibson started up the engine and left. It took ten minutes to get to Sidney. He parked on a side street and walked over to the bank. The entrance door was locked. He glanced at his watch and saw it was still relatively early. That's what they call banker's hours, he thought. He tapped on the glass to draw someone's attention. A teller turned and spoke to a person hidden from his view. The bank manager rounded the corner and scurried over. He flicked open the lock and ushered the detective in.

"Come in. I was going to call you," Jackson said.

He led Gibson to his office.

"Have a seat." Jackson gestured to the chair in front of his desk. "Any progress?"

"We're following several leads. I wanted to speak to Chelsea again," Gibson said. "I didn't see her at the counter."

"Chelsea?" His brows furrowed.

"Just some follow-up questions. Dianne was her friend, right?"

"I wouldn't know. But I believe Chelsea has gone on holidays for a few weeks." He pressed a button on the desk phone. "Could you come to my office, please?"

The receptionist rapped on the door frame. He had a blue suit on today. It was expensive looking, like the one he had worn on the previous occasion. He gave a fleeting glance toward the detective and shuffled uneasily. "Yes, sir. How may I be of help?"

"Hudson. Is Chelsea on holidays?"

"It was a family emergency. She said two weeks. But it could be longer if things got complicated." His smile never faltered. "I believe she went to Venezuela."

"Thank you." Jackson waved his hand to dismiss the man. He turned back to the detective. "Is there anything else I can assist you with?"

"Did you have time to look through Dianne's client list? Were there irregularities with any loans?" Gibson asked.

"No, no. Everything was legitimate. No problems at all."

"Have you met her husband?"

"Kevin. Yes. He attended several functions with Dianne."

"What was their relationship like?"

"Oh, my. I'm not sure I qualify to answer that. I noticed nothing out of the ordinary."

"No bickering or–" Gibson pressed.

"Nothing of the sort. They seemed a loving couple," Jackson interrupted.

"Did Dianne miss any days of work?"

"Never. She even came on weekends sometimes."

"I see." Gibson leaned forward. "How did she account for the bruises on her arms?"

"What? I don't understand what you mean," Jackson said. "I never saw any bruises. Oh. That explains why she always wore long sleeves. I didn't know."

A rap on the door made him stop.

"Come in," Jackson shouted.

"Here are those papers you asked for." The young girl placed the folder on the desk and turned to leave.

"You're a doll." He winked at her.

"I think that's it for today. Thanks for your time." Gibson stood up.

"Before you go." Jackson leaned forward. "On a personal note, I wanted to say I am interested in the project your son is working on. Very worthwhile undertaking. Please come by on Saturday to discuss a donation. Bring Katherine and Anatoe."

"That's very kind of you." Gibson reached over the desk and shook his hand.

He left the bank feeling as if he was missing something. Could Chelsea be the girlfriend? Kevin obviously knew the employees through his wife. His thoughts bounced back and forth. The sky had darkened, making it seem later in the day than it was. He gazed up to the clouds bunched into a large mass. They had taken on a deep grey hue. A light rain started with small drops and soon turned into a downpour. The detective ran to his truck and jumped in. He switched on the ignition so he could listen to a little music.

It wasn't only this case getting to him. He seemed to have lost his edge. There was a curious heaviness in his heart. He squinted into the rear-view mirror. The eyes that stared back were lifeless. Gibson wondered when he had surrendered his spark. Everything was so humdrum. Not something he could say to Katherine. She was in her glory. He needed to examine his own commitment. Where was this journey leading him? Should he turn in his badge for a different life? This one was becoming disagreeable to him.

Gibson started the engine and left for home. He stopped at a corner store and bought a bouquet of roses. The rain had slackened to a drizzle by the time he pulled into the driveway. He looked across the street toward the bay. The water was choppy with small whitecaps breaking on the shore. If the wind settled down overnight, he might get his kayak out at dawn. There was nothing to do except wait for someone to make a mistake.

* * *

The shrill of an alarm woke up the desk sergeant at the RCMP detachment in Sidney. A burly constable rushed into the foyer from the back.

"What the hell is going on?" The sergeant came round the counter to see outside.

"It's coming from the construction site next door," the constable said.

"Well, what are you waiting for? Move it."

The constable bounded down the steps and across the parking lot.

"Hey, you over there," he cried. "Police. Stop!"

Three kids looked up. Their brazen attitude had them ignoring the alarm, but a cop was another thing. They fled like whippets through the rubble. In five seconds, they'd hurled themselves over the two-metre fence. The darkness swallowed them up as they scampered down the street. Their footsteps blended into the sound of traffic.

The constable hung onto the metal barrier trying to catch his breath. The alarm stopped.

"You're getting old." The sergeant laughed and went back to his post.

"Should I write it up?"

"Did they take anything?"

"I don't think so."

"You better make a report anyway. Got anything else to do?"

"Not really."

"In triplicate," he yelled down the hallway.

"Yeah, yeah." The constable scowled.

Chapter 27

A flotilla of boats swept by, their sails fluttering in the gentle breeze. Close behind, a ski boat moved fast down the inlet. The foamy wake left in its path spread to the shoreline. Gibson steered his kayak into the wave. The water crested the bow, sending a fine mist into the air. To the west, the hills shimmered in the bright midday sunlight. Each stroke of the paddle glided him forward and eased his weary body. There was nothing to think about except the here and now.

Being alone on the water was daunting to some people. For Gibson, it gave him a sense of belonging. He explored the many tiny coves and let the hours drift by. The sun moved across the sky, dipped behind the first of the hills and cast a large shadow over the Saanich Inlet.

Gibson neared the dock and pulled his kayak out of the water. After securing it to the rack, he headed up the ramp. He walked across the street and to his house.

"Hello. I'm back."

Katherine yelled from the bedroom. "In here."

"What are you doing?"

"I can't decide what to do with my hair." She stared at him through the reflection in the mirror.

"You'll look great whatever you do." He kissed her neck and went through to the en suite bathroom. "Won't take me long to get ready."

"Are we picking up Anatoe?" Katherine asked.

"No. He'll meet us there."

* * *

The most direct route to North Saanich was by West Saanich Road. At the northernmost point, the road veered to the right and proceeded east. The tall fir trees shut out much of the remaining daylight. At that location, there were no streetlights to banish the dimness.

Gibson turned left when he saw the ornate wrought iron gates. The driveway meandered through a woodlot and then opened up to a vista of the sea. The house stood two-stories high with a widow's walk running the length of the roof. The white siding was stark against the backdrop of trees. At the entrance, water cascaded over the edges of a fountain into a marble pool. Victorian lampposts lined a flagstone path to a massive oak door with a lion's head knocker. The same ornate wrought iron embellished the hinges and doorplate.

"It should be a big cheque," Gibson said.

"Be nice." Katherine nudged him.

He pulled up to Anatoe's pickup parked in front of the three-car garage.

"Welcome." Jackson stood in the open doorway and waved them in.

"What a beautiful home," Katherine gushed.

Jackson grinned and led them through a hallway toward the back of the house. The dark wood wainscoting was enhanced by ivory-coloured walls. Gibson surveyed each room as they went by. The living room had leather couches facing each other in front of a massive hearth. The teak end tables had large antique lamps with crystal balls hanging from the shades. Luxurious Persian rugs were spread across wide plank hardwood floors. There was a rather messy laundry room. Farther on, the kitchen opened up to a grand room. The tinted glass doors to the sprawling terrace were pushed wide open, making the outdoors feel part of the indoor space. Across a big expanse of lawn, the ocean sparkled with the last beams of sunlight.

Anatoe greeted them when they entered the room.

"This is my wife, Lori," Jackson said. Mrs. Parker, standing behind the breakfast bar, tilted her chin. She had blonde hair over pale grey eyes that matched her tailored suit. A two-carat diamond ring was the only jewellery that adorned her fingers. But a diamond of equal size hung from a gold chain at the plunging neckline of her blouse.

Katherine took a seat by the opening. A surge of wind tousled her long brown hair. She pushed an errant strand behind her ear and turned away. Gibson sat in a wing chair, one of a pair by the fireplace. His son sat in the other. Lori fussed in the kitchen for several minutes before setting trays of finger food on the coffee table. She sat in a lovechair by a window, pulling on her pant legs to save the crease.

"Wine all round?" Jackson asked. He held up a bottle of red.

"None for me, thanks," Katherine stated.

"Would you prefer white?"

"We're having a baby. I..."

"Congratulations," Jackson said.

"Yes. Congratulations." Lori sat back in her chair and crossed her legs at the ankle.

Jackson got Katherine water and poured everyone else a generous portion of wine, draining the last bit out of the first bottle of the evening.

"Is this Chilean?" Gibson asked. He swirled the liquid in his glass.

"No. It's a BC wine."

"Very nice."

"Jackson goes to that wine store on Beacon," Lori said. "When he works late, he can rush down the street."

"I'll have to try that."

The small talk flowed into an easy conversation. Soon the topic turned to the purpose of their meeting, with Anatoe the centre of attention. He outlined his project and explained how it would go. His enthusiasm was infectious. He realized it was a big challenge, but he had great support from the community already. Jackson leaned forward with keen interest.

"We're in," Jackson said.

"Fantastic." Anatoe beamed.

"We were in before you got here." Jackson dipped into his pocket and took out an envelope.

Gibson nodded his head in appreciation.

"Should I open it now?"

"Yes. We can give more at a later date."

"Oh, my God. This is unbelievable." His eyes had sprung open at the enormous number.

The host served another round of beverages. The chatter was happier, looser. The lampposts in the courtyard switched on as the sunlight disappeared entirely. Lights twinkled in the distance from the islands across the open stretch of water. A warm breeze drifted into the room, bringing the salty aroma of the ocean with it.

"We should go," Gibson said.

They walked down the wide hallway to the front door. Coloured lights had transformed the fountain into a piece of art. Jackson waved as the two cars made their way up the curved driveway, their taillights disappearing into the shadows of the woods. At the road, Anatoe honked his horn as he swung left. Gibson headed back the direction they had come. As he cruised down the country lane, his mind was spinning with possibilities. He turned back to Katherine. She took his hand and squeezed gently. He almost poured out his thoughts, but something held him still.

***

Constable Grant was the desk sergeant at the Sidney RCMP station on Saturday night. He had a radio turned on low on the table behind him. He grabbed a handful of reports from the week before and flipped through them slowly. The jarring sound of the phone interrupted the quiet. He scooped it up and listened to the complaint with the instrument held away from his ear. The lady's voice shrieked two decimals above annoying. After promising he would send someone out to check out the noisy party, he hung up. He radioed to a patrol car in the area and went back to reading the reports.

Grant went through them rapidly. It had been a slow week thus far. The last report from the night before caught his attention. He yelled for the constable in the back to come up to the reception desk.

"Yeah. Is something going on?"

"Did I wake you up?"

"Ha. Ha."

"What did they steal?" Grant turned the paper on the counter to the constable and tapped at a section that hadn't been filled in.

"Nothing."

"Did you go over and take a look?"

"No, the gate was locked."

Grant pulled open a drawer and fumbled around its contents. He held up the key. "Guess you didn't know the construction boss left us this. Do you want to go now and take a look around? Check for damage. Just to be sure?"

"Okay." The constable grabbed the key and stalked out the door.

Grant could hear him rattling the chains holding the gates shut. A squeaking sound of worn steel on cracked concrete pierced his ears. He moved back indoors to wait.

The constable came back and tossed over a jacket.

"This is all I could find. It was by the bin where the kids were standing. It's not worth anything."

"No, but something tells me..."

"What?"

"It's a bomber jacket. My friend with the major crimes unit was looking for one of these."

"What the hell for?"

"It could be evidence. Let's bag it. Perhaps some of that dirt is blood."

Chapter 28

Gibson sat on a red metal patio chair on the front lawn. The sun had beat on it for a number of years and faded it to a pink colour. He peered through binoculars at the boats sailing down the narrow pass. The weather was perfect for a spin in his kayak. His phone buzzed in his back pocket. He had to slide forward to get it out.

"Gibson."

"Is this the detective?" The lady's pitch was high and squeaky.

"Paula." He hadn't recognized the number, but he knew the voice.

"You left your card. Said I could–"

"Of course. Anything I can do to help," Gibson interrupted. His heart flipped a beat. He felt something bad was coming.

"Ryder called. He wants to come home."

"What did you say?" Gibson hedged for time. He had an obligation as a peace officer. No getting around that simple fact! This could bite him in the ass. Why had he made her a promise?

"I told him he couldn't pretend he wasn't involved. Whether or not he did anything wrong." Paula paused.

"No matter what you said earlier. You can't make any guarantees. He has to face the consequences of fleeing the scene. Right?"

"I'll do everything I can," Gibson said. A sense of relief swept over him. "Will he turn himself in?" His phone purred again. A call on the other line. He ignored it completely. This was much too important. "Paula?"

"Would you be able to give us some time? So Ryder could clean up."

"You'll need to bring a lawyer," he answered.

"I don't have the money."

"Not to worry. I'll get you one," Gibson said. "Meet you in three hours at the Sidney RCMP. I'll be waiting in the lobby for you. I won't let you down."

"I know that. Thanks," Paula said.

When Gibson hung up, Katherine was standing in the doorway and asked, "Is it the boy?"

He turned toward her and nodded.

"If you believe in him, do your best."

"I will," he said and punched a number into his phone.

"Anatoe. I need your help."

"Anything."

They talked for several minutes. After Gibson ended the call, he dialled the number of the missed call.

"Grant."

"It's Gibson. I see you called. What's up?"

"We may have found your jacket."

"What? Oh. The bomber jacket?"

"Yeah. At the construction site next door. I'm just puzzled why Ryder would toss it there. But it's marked the same way the knife was. With the 'x's."

"Oh, shit. Ryder is turning himself in."

"When?"

"Today at noon. Anatoe will be there, too. He's bringing a lawyer."

"Oh, boy. What should I do with the jacket?"

"Send it to the lab," Gibson said. "Ask them to test it right away."

"Will do."

"Tell Jocko it's important."

"See you soon, Gibson."

"Thanks."

Gibson wondered why he wanted to help this boy so badly. Was it because he hadn't been there for Anatoe? He tried to rationalize it by telling himself he hadn't known about his son until this year. Although there had been clues he had brushed aside. But Anatoe had turned out all right. So why did he feel so wretched? Everything he thought and did was a back and forth struggle.

Gibson was sure Ryder wasn't involved. Now the jacket had put another kink in his reasoning. He only wished he could get some concrete evidence against Kevin. It was imperative to break his alibi. If not, would Ryder survive the allegations against him?

Gibson was too restless to wait around the house for the appointed hour, so he headed to Sidney. The streets were quiet, even for a Sunday morning, except down at the port. Boaters were setting out for a cruise through the Gulf Islands or over to Roche Harbor in the States. Lots of places to go to and enjoy. The water was like glass, not a ripple distorting the smooth surface. He parked in the RCMP lot and remained in his truck for a moment, jotting down a few notes in his book. He made a brief call to Constable Na.

* * *

Grant was sitting on a stool browsing through a magazine when Gibson entered the lobby. He put it aside at the sound of the door opening. "You're early." He glanced at the wall clock.

"Yeah."

"There's a room at the back. Last door on the right." Grant said.

"Thanks." Gibson headed down the hallway to the interview room. He dropped into a chair at the end of the table.

For the more serious part of an hour, Gibson drank in the quiet of the space, aware of the chaos that would fall upon them presently. He heard hurried footsteps and loud voices in the hall. There was a rap on the metal frame followed by the squeak of the door. Two men entered.

"This is Peter Tull," Anatoe said. "I'll be out front if you need me."

The attorney was a thin man with close-cropped hair and a very young clean-shaven face. He had on a short-sleeved shirt and khaki pants. Gibson extended a hand toward him. "Good of you to come on such short notice."

Peter nodded and plunked down his briefcase on the table. He scanned the room and picked a seat opposite Gibson to get comfortable. They chatted amiably for a few minutes. Then the room fell into an eerie stillness, leaving unspoken words to hang in the air. An occasional rustling of paper or cough went unnoticed. As the quietness grew deeper, Gibson shifted in his chair and peeped at his watch more than once. His heart grew heavier with every sweep of the minute hand. Would they show up? Now, he wasn't sure.

They arrived at around noon. Grant walked them down the corridor.

Ryder was dressed in spotless jeans and a tee shirt. There was a woven band on his slender wrist that he twirled in an endless circle. He was small, more childlike than a teenager. But his creased brows and tense face made him appear ten years older. His dark hair was neat and smelt fresh and fruity. He had earthy brown eyes that were cast down in a mournful gaze.

Paula had tamed her curly hair. Her shoulders were pulled down in frustration. She bit her lower lip to stop the quivering. A glassy layer of tears threatened to break the semblance of calm she portrayed.

"Have a seat," Peter said, indicating the two empty chairs beside him. "My name is Peter Tull. I will be representing you in the matter before us. This is Detective Gibson."

"I'll just step outside for a moment, so you can confer with your client."

"Thanks."

Gibson left the room and leaned on the wall in the hallway while he waited. Ten minutes went by before he was called back into the room. He took his seat again and looked around the room before speaking.

"Let's go through the events of that day," Gibson said. "Just tell me the truth, and we'll get through this."

"Okay," Ryder squeaked.

"Let's start with the knife you had in your possession."

Paula could hardly breath. This could have been a big mistake, coming here.

Chapter 29

"The knife?" Ryder asked. "What about it?" A smidgen of defiance seeped into his voice.

Peter's dark eyes shot up.

Ryder looked at him with wild-eyed desperation. All vestige of colour from his face had fled. He was like a trapped animal, brazen and fearful at the same time. The emotional pain reached out and stung them to the quick.

It stung Paula most of all. It felt as if she was treading cautiously on thin ice. At any minute, it could break and send her free-falling into a frosty demise. She refused to give up the struggle and reached out to her son.

"Where did you get the knife, Ryder?" Gibson asked.

"I bought the knife at a hardware store," Ryder said. "I was living on the street. I was scared."

"So it was brand-new."

"Yes."

"Did you ever have to use it?"

"No. I don't think I could have. It was just for show," Ryder said.

"Did you ever cut yourself with it?"

"No." He tilted his head at the weird question.

"We know it landed up at the Meadows' house," the detective said. He took another look at his notes. "Did you know that?"

"I suppose that's where I lost it. Only, I didn't know for sure." He broke off. "I meant to ask Virginia if she had it."

"It fell under the couch when the two of you were making out," Gibson said. He tried a little smile to quell Ryder's unease.

"But, how did it get, you know..." His eyes glazed over.

"We don't know exactly how your knife became the murder weapon." Gibson glanced over to Peter before he continued.

"Virginia told us that Dianne found the knife and put it in the shed. Someone stole it from there."

"Who?"

"If we knew that, we would know who the killer was."

"It wasn't me."

"Tell us what happened at the pier," Gibson continued.

Ryder exhaled and began his story. "I was headed to the hostel where I was staying a lot of the time. They're decent people there, and I felt safe enough. That night I took the path at the end of Beacon to cut through the skate park and across the lawn. Someone knocked into me like he was in a hurry."

"Did you get a look at the guy?"

"He was a big guy. He nearly bumped me off the sidewalk."

Gibson didn't think that sounded like Kevin. A big puff of wind would blow him over. He tried not to let his disappointment show.

"Would you recognize him again?" Gibson asked.

"I think so. Maybe."

"What happened next?"

"I kept on walking and decided to go down to the shore. For a toke." Ryder lowered his head and shrugged.

"Okay."

Paula stirred in her seat.

"Go on."

"That's when I saw someone lying on the ground. I could hardly believe my eyes. It was Virginia's mom. Then I saw the knife." Ryder stopped.

"Go on," Gibson prodded him.

"I picked it up. I knew it was mine." He stared at the wall.

Gibson knew he was reliving the nightmare.

"I tossed it away. I thought it went into the bay. Guess not."

"Why didn't you ring the police?"

"Are you kidding me? I was a goner." It was a vehement outcry in the quiet room.

It was moments before Ryder continued.

"Maybe I still am. But, I tell you, it wasn't me." He pressed his lips together to stop the tears that had welled up in his eyes. "What are you going to do to me?" He couldn't hold back his emotions in any longer and sobbed.

Paula squeezed her eyes shut.

Peter sat back in his chair.

"After we get a blood sample from you, we can compare it with the blood on the knife and on a bomber jacket we found," Gibson said.

"A jacket? How do you know it's mine?" Ryder whispered.

"You marked it the same as the knife."

"Oh."

"Why did you toss it in a bin next to the police station?" Gibson asked more out of curiosity than anything.

"I guess I wasn't thinking straight at the time. I was just in kind of a daze." Ryder blew out a deep sigh.

"We should get the blood results quickly. In the meantime, you'll have to remain here," Gibson said.

"In a cell?"

"I'm afraid so."

"But I thought..." Paula stammered.

"It's a process. I've spoken to Crown counsel. They know the circumstances."

"What does that mean actually?" Paula asked.

"They prefer to treat young offenders outside the prison system. We have the full support of the Youth Criminal Justice Act."

"Will they let Ryder go?"

"Let's not get ahead of ourselves," Gibson said. "Ryder will be comfortable here. No harm will come his way. Everything depends on the blood results." He slapped the table with his hand and stood up.

Everybody followed his lead except for Ryder. "I shouldn't have run away." The loud, heaving sobs punched Gibson in the gut.

***

After the desk sergeant took Ryder away, Paula left the interview room. The detective tried to reassure her, but she wasn't having it. She walked past the reception desk and out the door to her car without saying a word. The ride home was a blur. Her eyes had welled up with tears several times, but no tears came out. She sat on the porch well into the night thinking about her son, and how she had failed him. What was going to happen? The only thing she had left was hope. She had never prayed in her whole life, but as she sat in the dark, she pleaded to a higher power to save him.

***

It was a short hallway to a long night. Ryder sat on the lower bunk bed and closed his eyes. The fluorescent light in the hallway flickered through his eyelids. He lifted his head up and looked around. The walls were white, no graffiti or scribbles on the clean surface. He leaned back and laid down. The blanket was softer than he imagined it would be. He thought prison would be small, stinky cells with bars that rattled. It was pretty quiet here. No screaming voices, only the occasional ringing of a phone from far out. Even the bathroom had a division that gave some privacy. But it didn't matter. He knew he had screwed up royally this time. There were no more tears left in him, so he turned away from the light. All he had to do was let go of the darkness and drift off.

Chapter 30

A new day had started with a perfect dawn. Gibson had been sitting in the kitchen for two hours, watching as the first rays breached the horizon. Grey shadows were cast aside as the strong golden light spread across the mellow-blue sky. The warmth of the sun didn't dispel the dread that locked him in place. He took another sip of his coffee that had grown cold unnoticed. Today was going to be loaded with tension. Gibson stretched his back and went to the bedroom. Katherine made a soft snuffling noise and rolled over on her side. He dressed quickly, grabbed his badge and gun and blew a kiss into the air.

Gibson drove to the station and parked on Dallas Road. He scanned the street for Scottie's vehicle, but didn't see it. She would be here soon, with objections and acrimonious accusations. The DCs were sitting in their usual spots at his desk when he came into the room. Na looked up and grinned. It was sort of an apologetic smile. Not necessarily good news.

Gibson plopped into his chair, leaned back and stretched out.

"Bad night?" Na asked.

"Could be a worse day."

"What? Ryder or Scottie?" Gunner asked. He peered up from the magazine on his lap.

"Take your pick."

The elevator hummed as it started upward.

"Here she comes."

After a few minutes, the doors slid open. A step and a thud sounded as Scottie crossed the hall. She poked her head around the corner. "Are you guys talking about me?"

Na proceeded to stand up. Scottie waved her hand at him. "I can manage it." She hobbled into the room and wiggled her way into a chair, laying out the crutches against the desk.

"Welcome back," Gibson said.

"Are you sure? I heard rumours."

"Let's not jump to conclusions." Gibson said. Then he turned to Na. "Did you talk to George last night?"

"We did."

"Where's he been? Hiding from us?"

"No. Nothing like that. He went up island for a few days to visit his daughter and the grandkid."

"So, what did he have to tell you?" Gibson asked.

"He said technically he was teamed up with Kevin the night of the murder." Na paused. "But there was an emergency on a ship in dock. A burst water line. He was the only plumber on duty and spent the whole shift in the bilge. Didn't see anybody. He actually worked overtime and didn't get out of there until almost eleven the next day."

"Did you ask him if Kevin had a girlfriend?"

"He doesn't believe so. Gambling is Kevin's thing."

"Damn. I was counting on George giving us something." Gibson paused. "Let's move on. I got hung up yesterday at the RCMP station."

"Huh," Scottie snorted. She wasn't going to let it go without a fight. Ryder was her man. Gibson would have to convince her of his innocence.

"We also need to catch up with the yacht owner." He flipped through his notebook. "Hopkins. I was going to speak with him when he got back from his trip up north. Hopefully, he will shed some light on who was at that damn poker game."

"We could go there," Na said.

"All right. You and Gunner go to Canoe Cove," Gibson said. He studied his partner. She was rubbing her leg.

"It's still itchy." Scottie frowned. "I know I'm gonna be stuck with all the paperwork."

"You're on the mend. Can't be running around all over the place. You'll graduate to a cane before you know it."

"I'll be in my office." Scottie scowled. She skipped up on one foot, grabbed her crutches and left the room.

The DCs scooted out behind her. They scampered down the stairs, sounding overly loud for two guys.

Gibson sat back and stared at the ceiling, trying to empty his mind. The shrill ring of the telephone startled him. He reached over and plucked it up.

"Gibson."

"It's Jocko. You better come down to the lab."

He tore down the stairs two at a time. This was it, then. He walked down the long hallway. As he neared the doorway, he wondered if he should have called Scottie to come down. What was the matter with him, anyway? He pulled out his cell phone and called her.

"I'm headed for the lab. Come on down."

"Wait for me." Scottie hung up.

Gibson leaned against the wall until he heard the ding of the elevator. She stepped out and limped over. The grimace on her face told him to keep his smart comments to himself.

Jocko was sitting on a stool when they entered the room.

"What took you so long?" He looked at Scottie and said, "Sorry. You okay?"

She shot him a funny look.

The forensic lab technician strolled over to a counter and picked up the bomber jacket.

"I used Rapid DNA testing to get you results quickly. I do have a question though. Is this the jacket the suspect was wearing?"

"Yes, it is." Scottie smirked. She pointed at the x's on the collar. "Apparently, Ryder marks all his belongings that way."

Gibson saw what appeared to be blood on the right sleeve and sighed.

"Well, whoever wore this probably isn't the killer."

"What? That's bullshit," Scottie said. "There's blood right there." She pointed.

Gibson remained perfectly still.

"I would normally expect to see arterial spray from a carotid artery stabbing." Jocko paused. "Nothing is one hundred percent. But the odds are against the killer not getting splattered when a major artery is severed."

"But it could happen?" Scottie persisted.

"Like I said, it's not likely." Jocko turned the evidence bag to the dirty spot on the right sleeve. "The stain here is Dianne's blood." He held up a hand when Scottie tried to interrupt. "It's consistent with the kid's story. You told me he picked up the knife and threw it. The blood pattern here shows us that is likely what happened."

"What about the knife?" Gibson asked.

"Yes. The knife. It's not Ryder's blood in the hilt."

"Okay," Gibson said. "Thanks, Jocko."

The detectives left the lab. They rode the elevator together in silence.

"Come to my office."

They sat at Gibson's desk. He pulled a folder out of the bottom drawer and opened the transcript from the interview.

"Ryder was asked some specific questions about the knife to establish when blood transfer had happened." He scrolled down to the paragraph he wanted to read. "And I quote, 'I bought the knife at a hardware store. I was living on the street. I was scared. So it was brand-new. Yes. Did you ever have to use it? No. I don't think I could have. It was just for show. Did you ever cut yourself with it? No.'" He shut the file and stared at Scottie. "The unidentified blood can only be the killer's blood. Now we know it's not Ryder."

"Do we have a sample of Kevin's blood?"

"No."

"Can we get it?"

"Only if you ask nicely."

"He can refuse?"

"At this point, yes. He technically still has an alibi," Gibson said. "Although, we should put a lineup together and see if Ryder can identify him."

"Good idea. To tell you the truth, I'm glad to hear that it wasn't Ryder who killed Dianne."

Gibson looked up at her in surprise.

"The community would be in a panic if they thought kids could simply go round killing people for whatever." Scottie rubbed at her itchy leg. "This is driving me crazy."

"It means it's healing."

"Yeah, right."

"Let me call Crown counsel and give them an update. I think we'll be able to release Ryder to the Youth Justice Transition Services. It's something we talked about earlier. He didn't kill Dianne, but he did mess with the evidence."

"Will he do time for that?"

"Not likely. The whole point is to give young offenders the opportunity to contribute to the community. Not punish them."

"Paula will be relieved," Scottie said.

"Anatoe was hoping he could get Ryder enrolled in his program if he was eligible."

"That's sort of cool."

"I thought so, too." Gibson beamed and dialled a number. After being on the phone for ten minutes, he hung up. "It's a go."

"Okay. I'll drive." Scottie climbed out of her chair and shuffled out the doorway.

"Hey, not so fast."

"Ha. Ha. Just kidding."

They hopped into Gibson's truck.

"Call Paula."

There was no answer. After Scottie hung up, she asked, "Where are we going?"

"Call Grant. Paula's probably at the RCMP station," Gibson said. "They don't allow cell phones in the visiting area."

Scottie promptly called the police station. The desk sergeant picked up on the fourth ring.

"Is Grant around?"

"It's his day off."

"Is Paula there?"

"Who's this?"

"It's Scottie."

"Oh, hi there. Didn't recognize your voice. Paula is in the back with Ryder."

"Thanks. Gibson and I are on our way." She hung up.

"You get all that?" She turned to her partner.

"Yup."

"What about Anatoe? He would probably like to know what's going on."

"Right. Give him a shout."

The call went to voicemail, so she left a message. Gibson pulled into Sidney. Five minutes after, he parked the truck in the RCMP lot. The desk sergeant looked up when they entered the lobby.

"They're in the interview room," he said and pointed down the hallway.

"Did you receive the discharge papers from Bill Ward at Crown counsel?"

"For Ryder?"

"Yes."

"Not yet."

The fax machine lit up and spewed out a half-dozen pages.

"That'll be it."

The detectives marched down the corridor. Voices slipped out from under the closed door. Gibson swung it open and stepped into the room with Scottie bumping up behind him.

At the sound of the door, Paula looked up. Tears hung on her eyelashes. Her eyes crinkled at the corners. She had her arm wrapped around her son's shoulder. His body looked so small. He sniffed dejectedly and held his breath, fearful visiting time was up. He reached upward and took hold of his mother's hand.

Gibson held her gaze and grinned. "Ryder is free of the murder charge, but..."

A single tear rolled down Paula's cheek as she gasped for air.

"We'll have to work out the obstruction of justice," Gibson said. "He'll be fine."

Paula pulled Ryder in close, never to let go of him again. The soft weeping of the child in her arms crushed Gibson as no other experience in his life had done.

* * *

The moonlight cast a soft white glow through the small window. The blinds rattled with the fresh breeze that blew in, so unlike the stale air of the cell. As midnight approached Ryder lay on his narrow bed at home, unable to sleep. An owl hooted in the tall cedar on the boulevard. He buried his head into the fluffy pillows. The familiar smell of his mother's perfume lingered on the quilt. He gave the once over around his room. Everything was just as he had left it. The desk was stacked high with books, his music player, and a refurbished laptop. A scuffed backpack leaned against the wall where he had tossed it earlier. The posters on the walls had hung there for his entire life. He turned the clock on his nightstand so he could see and pushed the light. It was later than he realized. He pressed into the mattress and shut his eyes.

The door hinges squeaked as his mother entered from her vigil on the porch. He listened as she walked through the house. The sound of water running in the pipes made him think she was in the kitchen. As the silence settled again, he heard crying in the next room. He got up and searched the closet for his treasured mementos. The scrape of the wood was loud as he pulled a box off the top shelf. He froze, tuning his ears to the hallway. There was nothing amiss, so he sat back on his bed. He flicked through the contents, fingering each picture, each ticket stub, each keepsake. The stuff his mother and he had shared. All shattered by the unintentional disclosure of who his actual father was.

His first reaction had been to run away. Who could he trust? Who could he talk to about that? It was a betrayal of huge proportions to him. And who was Guy to him? Her lover. A fake dad.

He believed he was alone in his pain, but he was wrong. Despite how it had looked, he knew his mom had always been there for him. As he held his baby photo, a new worry seized his fragile mind. Was he himself capable of bad things because he had the same genes as a rapist? He closed the box and set it aside. His eyes became heavy. He refused to let the unnamed man's crime keep him from succeeding in life.

Chapter 31

Quick moving clouds, tinged a greenish purple, pushed up and over the distant hills. The flag atop the building across the street billowed in the cool breeze. Leaves shifted along the lane in tiny tornado formations. The salty smell of the ocean was strong. A change was coming. Not only in the weather, but in everything around Gibson. He could feel it in his bones, the weighty sensation of water pressing down on him. Yesterday's positive outcome should have made him feel exalted. But the relief didn't come, only an ill mood, made worse by an unexplained anxiety that thwarted him.

As Gibson drove down the highway to Sidney, his mind leaped from one matter to another. Someone up ahead tossed a cigarette out of their car window. Its lit end sent sparks along the tarmac, then died before it tumbled into the dry grass on the shoulder.

He took the back way into town, so he could cruise along the waterfront. There were tons of people walking dogs or pushing baby buggies. A slew of kids on bikes and skateboards were hanging around the park. He steered into the RCMP car lot and headed to the courthouse around the corner.

Scottie was milling around the courtroom area when he entered the foyer. The stench of sweat, stale breath, and coffee emanated from the people seated on hard wooden seats.

The detectives passed by and headed down a wide corridor leading to the judge's chamber. Anatoe leaned against the wall with his arms folded over his chest. A large manila envelope was gripped in his hand. They greeted each other in low murmurs. A door opened across the hall. A young woman ushered them into an enormous room and scampered off. The well-appointed space was filled with antique furniture and innovative electronics. A massive desk stood in front of a floor-to-ceiling bookcase. Three wing chairs and an overstuffed leather couch circled an ornate coffee table. A sideboard held a collection of glassware and a large jug of water. The fireplace in the corner had a stone mantle covered with framed photographs. The gleaming polished wood of the walls had the sweet scent of freshly squeezed lemons.

"Should we sit while we wait for the rest of them?" Scottie asked.

Anatoe plopped down on the sofa and placed his folder on the table. He pressed his lips tight to keep from smiling and formed a steeple with his fingers. The detectives each picked a winged chair. A few minutes passed by before they heard footsteps, then voices. Suddenly the door swung open. Ryder stood with his hands at his sides, his gaze ping-ponging around the room. Paula gave him a gentle prod. He moved toward Anatoe and sat down. Peter Tull, Ryder's lawyer, strode in and gave a wave to Gibson. He sat on the arm of the couch with his legs crossed at the ankle.

Bill Ward from the Crown counsel popped his head into the room.

"Is everyone here?" A playful grin made his eyes sparkle. He turned to someone in the hallway. A clacking of shoes along the tile floor faded away. He went toward the window and stared out onto the green lawn.

A whoosh from the back of the room made everyone turn. A tall, black-haired man strode through a door concealed by the bookcase. After a cursory nod, he sat in the chair beside Scottie. His shoulders were drawn backwards, and his head held high. The judge hiked his robe up, exposing his slip-on Hush Puppies. He leaned forward and placed his hands on his thighs.

"Welcome. Thanks for expediting this process for us, Bill." Judge Fred Saunders turned to Ryder. "How are you doing, young lad?"

Ryder gave him a hangdog look.

"Don't be afraid of me." He laughed and tugged at his robes. "It's for show."

"I'm okay."

"Good. Good." He sat back in his chair. "Everything is set. We're all on the same page?"

"Yes, your Honour," Anatoe said.

"You have the paperwork?"

"Yes." He stood up and passed the folder to the judge.

"We need everybody to sign, and then it's official," Saunders said. "The offense here was quite minor compared to some things I have to deal with, so we moved quickly to clear this up."

"Thank you, your Honour," Peter said.

"Let me give you a summary in terms you can understand, Ryder," Saunders said. He met the boy's gaze. "Given the evidence we have, we are all in agreement that you were not involved in the murder of Mrs. Meadows. Although you did interfere with the evidence by throwing the knife away. Now the Crown has discretionary power to pursue charges or not. We felt it wasn't in the public interest to go down that route." He paused. "Do you follow this so far?"

"Yes, sir." His meek voice was hardly audible in the cavernous room.

Paula held onto her son's hand.

"All right. But we need to do something. It's not punishment, but something to help you move forward in your life. Apparently, you have a good friend in Anatoe. He was instrumental in providing us with a good solution. He's working with the youth justice system to set up shop, teaching mechanic skills. Is that something that interests you?"

"Yes, sir." Ryder's eyes lit up.

"Great. That's all we really need to know. Let's get these papers signed. I have a courtroom to go to." Saunders laughed again. "I like happy endings." He wrote his usual scribble on the forms and stood up. "Good luck."

"Thank you, sir," Ryder said. He pressed his lips together, so he wouldn't embarrass himself by crying.

The judge left the room by the same concealed door. A collective sigh sent everyone into a titter. A relaxed grin crossed Gibson's face. Paula placed a palm over her heart. Her smile was small and fleeting as if she couldn't believe everything would be fine. A light flush dotted her cheeks. It was the first time Gibson had seen any colour in her ghostly pallor.

"Lunch anyone?" he asked. "The lawyer pays."

Peter jabbed the detective in the arm.

* * *

It had been a long day. Gibson was all alone in the office, his head clouded with questions. He swivelled his chair, stretched out his legs and laced his fingers behind his head. His tense muscles loosened minimally. Everything had gone well with Ryder. That he was happy with. His uncertainty was about his ability to do the job.

Na had been in touch to let him know that Hopkins hadn't shown up at the marina yet. Gunner said the sailboat had probably been delayed by a storm that was sweeping in farther north. It had lashed the west coast of

British Columbia with gale force winds and rain for two days. Gibson figured he would go by in the morning and sort it out. If they ever showed up at all.

He had no other pressing business, so he locked up and went home.

***

Katherine sat in the living room in an overstuffed chair with a mug of steaming tea on the end table. A book lay upside down on the throw blanket folded over her knees. Muted voices from the television played in the background. The finches, cuddled together in the corner of their cage, were having an afternoon nap.

Gibson tiptoed past and headed down the hallway. After a refreshing shower, his nose led him to the kitchen.

"Are you sneaking around the house?" Katherine asked. She stood in the doorway. "Did it go well?"

"Couldn't be better," he answered.

"Why do you look so down?"

"It's been stressful."

"Have you eaten?" Katherine asked.

"Yes. But I have to say, I smell something awesome cooking."

"Lasagna. Your favourite."

"You're a doll. When will it be ready?"

"Another hour."

"Time for me to go across the street? Check out my kayak."

"Sure." She waited by the door as he headed for the dock. "Don't be late," she shouted.

Gibson walked down the ramp to wooden docks that stretched out into the water. Various sized boats were tied up. Most were cruisers or ski boats. The sailboats were anchored out in the bay. He pulled his kayak off the rack and wiped it down with a rag. As he polished the fibreglass hull, he thought about where the case was going. It was basically stalled unless they could break Kevin's alibi. That would give them access to his DNA and fingerprints. There was no way Kevin would give these up voluntarily. He was adamant he was guiltless of any misconduct. That was worth a laugh. Gibson was convinced domestic violence had been a large part of Dianne's life and ended with her dying.

All they needed was the blood on the hilt, or the partial print to be Kevin's. Or better still – both. There were no other motives. There were no other suspects. Suddenly it came to him that speaking to Hopkins was imperative. Was he a friend of Kevin and avoiding the detective? No, he didn't imagine anyone would want to be implicated in a murder cover-up. The bad thought came and went.

Gibson decided he would stand on the dock all day tomorrow if he had to. He finished up and headed back home.

Chapter 32

Expensive cars queued up along the circular driveway. Gibson spun his truck around the fountain and parked further up the hill. He held onto Katherine's hand as they strolled back to the house. As the hosts, the Parkers stood in the lobby and greeted the patrons as they came in. Jackson wore a black suit, white shirt, and black patent shoes that matched his wife's black and white sequined outfit.

"We're going to bring the bucks in tonight," Jackson said. "We haven't had such a large turnout for a fundraiser, since when I don't know."

"This is fantastic. Anatoe will be so pleased."

"Have fun. We'll talk later." Jackson turned to embrace the next person.

Gibson and Katherine moved through the hallway to the grand room. Guests mingled and sipped champagne. The ladies wore chic dresses and glittering jewellery. The men had tailor-made suits and Rolex watches. Not quite a black-tie affair but close. Waiting staff dressed in white with black sashes around their waist carried trays of drink and slipped unobtrusively through the crowd. Voices drifted into the room from the people outside.

They stepped out onto the patio. There was a buffet counter set up at one end, with an ice sculpture of a car. Tables covered in white cloths were spread across the lawn. The perfumed smell of flowers floated along by the faint breeze. Gibson spotted Anatoe milling about and shaking hands. He knew a few employees from the bank, as well.

Gibson placed his hand at the small of Katherine's back and pointed her to an empty table. Close by a quartet played classical music.

"This is posh," Gibson said.

"Isn't it?" she replied.

Jackson strolled up to a dais on the terrace. The music stopped abruptly.

"Thank you for coming. And for supporting our youth," the host said. "I can't express how important all these programs are. So dig in deeper than usual tonight. I know everyone here is very generous, and I want to thank everyone in advance for their help. That's all I have to say. Enjoy the evening."

After the clapping died down, the band took up a merry tune. Jackson stepped away from the microphone and blended into the crowd. The chatter became louder as people began to intermingle, catching up with old friends and meeting new ones. Occasionally, the warm air was punctuated by hoots of laughter.

Gibson headed to the buffet. He picked up two plates from a tall stack and cutlery from a basket. The sun filtered down through the trees and threw the first shadows of the approaching dusk. Tiki torches glowed orange in the dimming light. As Gibson waited his turn, he scanned the lawn and spotted Chelsea, the head teller from the bank. He wondered when she had returned from her trip. He was tempted to rush down and interrogate her, but common sense made him stay in the line. The sputtering of burgers on the grill drew his attention. Citronella candles mixed with the wood smoke wafted around the terrace. He made it back to the table without dropping anything.

"I'll be right back," Gibson said as he put the plates down.

"I don't know if I can eat much so soon." Katherine stared at him as he walked away.

Gibson strode up to the bank teller and said, "Hello, Chelsea. May I have a word with you?"

She tilted her head and frowned.

"I'm Inspector Gibson. I spoke to you at the bank, about Dianne."

"Of course."

"I'm really sorry to approach you just now about this, but I haven't been able to reach you."

Chelsea remained quiet. She glanced at her partner.

"Can I ask you about Dianne? You mentioned her family life."

"I only know what Dianne hinted at."

"And what's that?"

"Kevin abused her. Beat her."

"I see," Gibson said. "Do you think that led to her death?"

Chelsea lifted her head and stared into his eyes. "I couldn't say. All I know is she was afraid of him." She hesitated. "Dianne was seeing someone."

"She was having an affair?"

"I think so."

"Who?"

"Someone at work."

"Did you see something?" Gibson asked.

"No." Chelsea shrugged. "It's just a feeling I have."

Gibson nodded his head. "Thank you." He walked back to the table and plunked into his chair. He didn't need to ask Chelsea if she was involved with Kevin. Her partner was a woman.

"What was that about?" Katherine asked.

"Nothing."

"Eat. Your food is going cold."

Gibson took a bite of his burger and chewed slowly, mulling over what Chelsea had said. This was the first time anyone had offered confirmation that Dianne may have suffered domestic abuse at the hand of Kevin. Even Virginia had acted skittish around her father. Was there more to find out? And who the hell could Dianne have been having an affair with? He racked his brain, trying to think of all the male employees that worked at the bank. He swept his eyes toward the house. Paula stood on the patio, her eyes roaming over the grounds. She fixed her gaze on him. The pensive melted into recognition. Gibson gestured to her. Paula hesitated before stepping forward. She stood awkwardly at the table, pressing her hands down her plain cotton dress. Her cheeks were flushed with embarrassment.

"Have a seat. Meet my wife," Gibson said.

There was something in the way Katherine smiled at you that was calming.

"Your husband has been so kind to us," Paula said.

"Is Ryder coming?" Katherine asked. She touched Paula's hand.

"He wasn't certain he should. He went out on his bike." Paula sighed and sat back. The conversation flowed easily as they chatted, mostly about Anatoe and his involvement with the youth services.

* * *

The last rays of the late afternoon sun fell through Ryder's window. His mom had just left for the fundraiser. He lay on his bed and stared at the clouds as they dipped in and out of his view. A tightness in his throat that had persisted since his night in jail made it difficult to swallow. He shuddered at the memory, closing his eyes against the numbness of it all. Anxiety grabbed at him. He could no more turn off his conflicted emotions as alter the truth. As hard as he tried, he worried about the future. Ryder steadied his heartbeat. He daydreamed of a perfect life where stormy moments didn't exist.

Sunlight played on his eyelids. Ryder tilted his head to the warmth. A surge of courage swept over him. He bounded off the bed and out of the house. He jumped on his bike and pedalled until his legs ached. There was a fresh sense of freedom as he rode through the streets and tracks he knew well. He felt nothing could go wrong now. It simply couldn't.

When he got to the Parkers', a fleeting moment of doubt took hold of Ryder as he gazed over the grounds in search of his mom. When he caught sight of her, his heart swelled.

* * *

"Hey, there's Ryder now," Gibson said and waved him over.

Ryder flopped into a chair and crossed his arms. He sat still for a few minutes before springing up. "Can I talk to Anatoe?" he asked in a pleading tone. "Don't worry. I'll ride my bike back."

Paula pressed her lips together tightly. "All right. Only don't be too long. It's already growing dark."

"Okay, Mom." He sauntered across the lawn and vanished.

* * *

Anatoe sat at a big table in the far recess of the yard. He was tilting forward with his elbows resting on the tabletop. It was obvious that he was loving the spotlight. Ryder hesitated momentarily before approaching the crowd gathered around the guest of honour. He had to wedge in-between two rather large people to make it to the front.

Anatoe turned to the right, and their eyes met. If it was anyone else Ryder would have dropped his gaze. He felt a connection with the guy. It was someone who believed in him. Hope hugged Ryder. The following hour was one of the happiest of Ryder's life. He was a part of something, something big and wonderful. As the daylight dwindled to a dusky gloom, the crowd thinned.

* * *

They continued to talk as the sky darkened.

"Thank you for everything," Paula said. She rose from her chair. "It's my bedtime."

"I'm glad you came," Gibson said.

They sat quietly after Paula left, listening to the music. The stars began to emerge slowly, one at a time appearing like beacons against the black sky.

"Oh," Katherine muttered and clutched her belly.

Gibson turned to her, apprehension in his eyes.

"Are you okay?"

"I'm not sure."

"It's been a long day for you," he said. "Perhaps we should go."

Gibson stood up, preparing to leave. The bank receptionist scurried over to their table. He glanced around before he shoved a note into the detective's hand. His voice crackled as he spoke, "You can call me." He took off as fast as he had arrived.

Katherine grabbed at her husband's wrist. Gibson tucked the paper in his jacket pocket. As he gazed after the man, he spotted Kevin standing with a group of people. Katherine's nails dug into his skin. He turned back to her slowly.

* * *

Ryder took his leave with the anticipation of good things to come. An optimism shattered moments later. He crossed the terrace and walked into someone blocking the door. When he looked up, he stared into the killer's eyes. The shock made him take a step backward. Fear snatched his guts. The man spoke first. Ryder fled with the words rolling in his head. Not sure where to turn to, he raced down the steps toward Gibson. He almost tackled the detective in his rush to get away.

"I saw the guy..." Ryder's breathing was erratic as if he had run a marathon.

"Not now," Gibson said briskly.

"But..." he sputtered. The bitter taste of blood filled his mouth as he bit down on his lips.

"Sorry, Ryder. We'll talk about this tomorrow. Katherine's ill."

"Okay." He shrugged and peeked over his shoulder.

Ryder ran back up the stairs and out the front door. As he rode away on his bike, he gritted his teeth with determination. His legs pumped with a furious motion as he headed down the road—no streetlighting to pave his way. The canopy of trees outlined against the sky shut out any light. Even the stars and moon couldn't breach the dimness ahead. A movement in the gathering darkness froze his heart. A deer darted across the lane and scurried into the underbrush.

He zoomed up the overpass to get over the highway and hit the trails. Dusk was quickly fading into night. The path in front of him vanished into an inky blackness. He burst out of the woods into his street. The streetlamps made garish yellow puddles of light on the pavement. A car moved up the road behind him and passed. Another circle of headlamps on full beam cruised behind him, but followed slowly. The glare shone in his mirror. Panic ripped through Ryder. He knew what the man wanted. With an additional push, his house came into sight. Another few paces, he saw his mother on the porch. Her lit cigarette zigzagged in the shadows.

Ryder felt the crush of metal as the car hit his bike. His mom stood up. Their eyes locked briefly. There was the screech of tires, and then nothing.

Paula screamed and screamed.

The car raced away.

* * *

"Come on." Gibson steadied Katherine as they worked their way to the vehicle.

She let out a small shriek.

"I'm taking you to the hospital." Gibson wasn't sure what was going on, but he knew it wasn't going to be good. He raced down the main road. His heart was beating in his throat. Katherine had slumped into her seat. Her face had gradually turned pale. At the entryway, he took hold of a wheelchair. He gently lifted her into the seat. There was some blood.

The next hour was mostly a blur. Gibson sat in the waiting area. He stood up, then sat down. Scottie ran into the room.

"What's going on?"

"She lost the baby." He closed his eyes and let out a sob.

Chapter 33

The doctor said miscarriages in the first trimester were more common than most people thought. He said Katherine would be herself in a few days with plenty of rest. Gibson knew that wasn't true. She would never be fine again. This would mark an end to her sanity. But for now, she was tucked in bed at home with a couple of pills to help her sleep. He sat in a chair beside her and watched her drift into a restless slumber. He had attempted to take her hand, but she shook it away. Her rebukes to his attentiveness were disheartening.

He sighed deeply and slipped out of the room, searching for solace in a dram of whiskey. He poured a large measure into a crystal tumbler and sank into his favourite chair. The quiet was nearly absolute as Gibson sat in the dimly lit room. The silence of the night was broken only by the occasional hoot of an owl and the screeching of tires in the distance. He dozed off for an hour or so, waking with a start. The vivid dream vanished when he opened his eyes. Unable to sit still, he got up and left the house, shutting the door gently behind him.

Gibson hopped into his truck and headed to Victoria. Few vehicles were out and about at four in the morning. It was rarely he found himself driving with no intention and no destination. He cruised around the waterfront on Beach Drive and came upon Dallas Road without meaning to. The lights of the glass and concrete building were a stark contrast against the black sky. Across the street, the dock lights were almost blindingly bright.

He parked on the road and trudged up the steps to the door. With his key card, he let himself in. The coolness of the foyer felt nice against his hot skin. He halted in front of the lift and pushed the button. The doors slid open immediately. He was obviously the only person around. The ride up to the second floor took five seconds. He stepped into the hallway and walked to his office. After unlocking his door, he flipped the light switch. He tried to remember the last time he was in his office. There was another pile of bulletins on his desk. A few folders as well. But Gibson wasn't interested in any of it.

He strolled over to the window and gazed at the mountains in the distance. The moon had almost reached the western horizon and would soon disappear from sight. He couldn't watch the sunrise from here, but a faint glow crept into his peripheral vision. Suddenly, he realized he had been driving around for over two hours.

He turned away from the window and sat at his desk. The bottom drawer was still pulled out, so he rested his feet and leaned back into his chair. He hoped the coffee shop across the street opened early. A sudden dryness in his mouth had made him long for some coffee. He checked his jacket pocket for a mint or something to quench the discomfort. His fingers touched a crumpled-up piece of paper. As he unfolded the note from the bank receptionist, he realized he hadn't changed his suit from the evening's event. He read, 'I think Dianne was having an affair. Hudson.'

Gibson picked up the phone, and then replaced it in its cradle. It was too early to call anyone. He leaned back into his chair. Chelsea had told him the same thing, but she had been more explicit in the details. There had been a flurry of activity just before their departure from the Parkers' house. Spotting Kevin among the bank employees had been a surprise. But it was probably normal to invite him. Wasn't it? And what did Ryder say? What were his exact words, again? 'I saw the guy.' Was that it? Or was it 'I saw Guy'? Did that make sense? Yes, if Guy had something to do with Dianne's death. Gibson shook his head. No, no. That was stupid. Ryder knew what Guy looked like, so he couldn't have been the person at the pier.

Gibson pulled out a drawer and grabbed a folder. He flipped the pages until he came to the list of bank employees. The only name that popped out at him was Jackson. He leaned back in his chair again and thought about the manager. That could make some sense. Dianne was having an affair with Jackson. Kevin found out and being the violent man that he was, he killed her. He needed to ask Ryder if he had ever met Dianne's husband. If he didn't know what Kevin looked like, could he have been the person on the pier? He really didn't have a clue what Ryder had wanted to say, so he needed to just ask him.

Gibson dialled Paula. The phone rang ten times and went to voice mail. He left a message for her to call back right away. It was very important that he should speak with Ryder. He turned his head at the sound of footsteps in the hallway.

Scottie peeped around the doorway.

"Hi," she chirped.

The inspector greeted her without smiling.

"May I come in?" Her voice was quieter, less sure.

Gibson stood up quickly. "Let's get a coffee. I think the café must be open by now."

Scottie opened her mouth to say something. The expression he gave stopped her. A heavy silence fell over them as they walked down the steps, out the building and across the street.

The coffee shop was abuzz with people. They found a small table in the corner and sat. The glare from the streetlamps lessened as the sky brightened. Then the lights blinked off in unison. Gibson stared out the window and watched as the parking lot filled with vehicles. Some people headed toward the coffee shop. Others strolled over to the dock area. He figured most were workers this early in the morning.

Scottie waited, sipped her latte and munched on a cinnamon roll.

"Ryder tried to tell me something last night, but I had to rush away."

Scottie didn't say anything.

"Let's get Kevin picked up and put him in a lineup. See if Ryder recognizes him as the man on the sidewalk."

"You bet," Scottie said. "Should I get Na and Gunner on that?"

"Yes."

They sat for a few more minutes before Gibson spoke again.

"Hudson said Dianne was having an affair."

"Hudson?"

"From the bank."

"The dandy?"

"Yeah." Gibson grinned. "You have a way with words." He gave her a run-down on his thoughts.

"So we really need to speak to this Hopkins fella," Scottie said.

"That was my plan earlier. Now, I think it is even more important. He could make or break Kevin's alibi."

"Let's go to Paula's house first. I can't get a hold of her or Ryder. There's something…"

"OK, let's go." Scottie sucked back the last of her drink and stood up. She clutched at her leg and winced.

"Still sore?"

"A little. The cane helps. I hated those crutches."

The drive to Sidney took less than thirty minutes. Gibson pulled up to the house and knocked on the door. There was no answer.

"What do you think?"

"Call her," Scottie said.

Gibson dialled the number. They could hear the phone ringing inside.

"Don't you have her cell number?"

"Yeah, I do now. Let me try that."

Paula didn't answer even as he let it ring and ring.

"Should we go to the marina, and then we can come back?" Scottie said.

"Sure."

Gibson drove to Canoe Cove and parked in a designated spot for visitors. Boats cruised out of the bay, headed for a sail or a day of fishing. Bright yellow water taxis zipped back and forth from the numerous tiny islands. The cry of seagulls faded in and out with the breeze. Not to be outdone, the sound of drills and buffers added to the mêlée as workers toiled in the dusty yard.

The detectives walked to the end where the larger vessels moored. Bare masts reached into the sky, their rigging rattling against the aluminum. The tallest of them towered metres over the rest at Dock F. Midway up the mast, a radar unit reflected the sunlight. They walked slowly down the ramp with Scottie lagging behind and approached the yacht. The size of it was pretty staggering. Billionaire row. Na almost got it right.

A short, stylish man with a bright white shirt, Bermuda shorts, and canvas sneakers leaned on the stainless-steel railing.

"Good morning, detectives," he said.

"You must be Hopkins," Gibson replied.

"Yes. I heard you'd been looking for me. Come aboard."

They clambered up to the cockpit and sat down on thick vinyl cushions.

"It's about our little poker game," Hopkins said. His grin widened, with dimples. "Perfectly harmless."

"I'm sure," Gibson said. "Do you know Kevin Meadows from the ferry terminal?"

"I sure do."

"You know his wife was murdered," Gibson said.

"Yes. What a terrible thing. Poor guy."

Gibson pulled out his notebook and gave Hopkins the date and time of the murder. "Was there a poker game that night?"

"That was a Thursday. Right?" Hopkins asked.

"Yes, it was."

"We do have a regular game for Thursday evenings. It starts at six and can go on all night."

"Was Kevin there on that night?"

"Let me think. Kevin is a regular. That was just before my trip up north." Hopkins rubbed at his chin. "Yes, he was there, but I can't give you a precise time. He usually shows up around ten and stays for a couple of hours. It's his lunch hour. So he says."

Gibson glanced sideways at Scottie.

"Could you be more precise on the time?"

"Sorry. That's the best I can do," Hopkins said.

"Is there anything that could jog your memory? Do you keep a record of winnings or anything like that?"

"No, no. Nothing like that."

"Thanks for your help."

The detectives strolled back to the vehicle.

"That was a bust. Let's go to that pub for a coffee. Or something to eat sounds good."

They sat along the rear terrace and ordered hamburgers. Gibson's cell rang just as he was going to phone Paula again.

"Gibson."

"It's Constable Grant."

"What can I do for you, Grant?"

Scottie glanced up at the mention of her friend from the RCMP detachment.

"I thought you should know there was a hit and run last night."

Gibson's eyebrows shot upward. He waited for the rest.

"In front of Paula's home. It's Ryder." The constable paused. "He's in a coma."

"Oh, shit. Thanks for calling." Gibson hung up. He lowered his head and rubbed his temple.

"What?" Scottie asked.

"No wonder I couldn't reach Paula. Ryder was struck by a car, and he's in the hospital."

"Is it bad?"

"Real bad."

* * *

The hospital lot was full, so Scottie parked in the emergency area. She left her flashers on, hoping she wouldn't get towed away. They walked through the crowded waiting room to the front entry. A different lady was at the receptionist counter. She directed them down a long corridor to the intensive care unit.

Scottie stayed in the hallway. She sat in a chair and made some calls. Gibson tapped on the door before going in.

Ryder's head lay heavily on the pillow. His face was pale against his wispy dark hair. A monitor beside him blipped steadily. The IV dripped fluid down a clear tube to his arm. The patient chart hanging at the base of the bed had scribbled marks down half the page.

Paula was sitting erect in a chair beside her son. Her eyes were closed.

There were two empty chairs in the corner. Gibson sat in one and quietly waited, unsure exactly what he could say to make things better. Probably nothing at all. He tried to imagine being in the same situation, but he couldn't. Not even close. He wasn't even sure if Ryder would make it.

But then again, Ryder was young and resilient. Why was he being so negative? He watched Paula as her lips moved, as if in prayer and wished he knew how to find some meaning to it all.

"My baby. He hasn't stirred since I got here."

The broken silence startled the detective. He had questions. Should he ask now?

"Could you tell me what happened?" Gibson leaned forward.

"You know I left early last night before you guys. Ryder stayed to hang out with Anatoe. Well, you know all that part. It's what happened next that you want to know."

She stopped and bit her lip.

"I was sitting on the porch having a smoke. I do that a lot. Sometimes it's just to relax. Other times, I wait until Ryder comes home. You know. From a movie or whatever boys do at his age. I never really worried about him. It was just a habit. I have to say, I did spend a lot of time on the porch over the last few weeks because… well he ran off, didn't he? Then I really had something to worry about. Anyway, I saw someone hightailing it down the street. I knew it was Ryder straight away because one of the lights on his bike has a loose connection and it flickers. I put out my smoke and stood up to go inside. I knew he was safe at that point. Then I noticed a car following close behind him. Too close. I thought the person had plenty of room to pass. I couldn't figure out what he was doing." She let out a small sob. "And then the man just ran him over."

Gibson listened to Paula pour out her heart.

"So you saw it was a man. Do you know who he was?"

Paula just shook her head.

The clacking of shoes drifted in from the hall. A phone rang shrilly for several moments before it was answered.

"What about the vehicle? What can you tell me?"

She shrugged.

"Was it dark or white…"

"I don't know," Paula raised her voice, then burst into tears.

Gibson sat quietly for another minute, but her sobs never relented. He stood up and quietly left the room.

Out in the hallway, Scottie stared at him. "Well. Did she see anything?"

"She says no, but I think she knows who it was."

"Why wouldn't she tell you?"

"Not sure," Gibson said, and shrugged.

Chapter 34

Gibson was absolutely furious. The constables had been sent to find Kevin the night before, but he was nowhere to be found. He wasn't at work, at home, or at the poker game. Even Virginia was missing.

The inspector stared out the window and watched a cruise ship coming into the dock. He was so tired, his head was spinning. Katherine had refused to talk about anything. After a brief argument, he had landed up on the couch. Both his neck and shoulder hurt from the various awkward positions he found himself in as he tried to get comfortable. All he managed to do was toss and turn most of the night. So not only was his mind bent out of shape, but his body ached, as well.

Gibson turned toward the sound of boots hammering up the steps. Gunner struck the door frame with a thud.

"Sorry, boss. We got Kevin."

"Where?"

"At the Sidney RCMP building. He's in the drunk tank." The constable laughed.

"Where are Scottie and Na?"

"They were prowling the town hunting for Kevin most the night. Na went home," Gunner said.

"And Scottie?"

"She's waiting for you in Sidney. I was sent here to get you."

"All right. Good. Let's go."

Gunner drove at the speed limit, but he tended to jump off the line when the light turned from red to green. It made for an uncomfortable ride, something like his night on the couch. Gibson downed a couple of more painkillers and leaned back into the seat. They got to Sidney fairly quickly because the rush hour was headed in the opposite direction. Gunner parked the vehicle just as a sprinkle of rain began to fall. Gibson looked up to the sky. He saw some mean black clouds gathering in the east and headed straight for them. They entered the lobby before the downpour took hold. Grant greeted them at the counter.

"They're in the last interview room."

"Thanks."

Gibson and Gunner hurried down the corridor. They could hear shouting coming from the back.

"Who the hell do you think you are?" Kevin yelled. His boisterous voice thundered through the steel door. "I demand to be released."

Suddenly the door swung open. Kevin stopped short of running into the inspector. "Get out of my way." He raised a hand to push Gibson aside.

Gunner came up behind his boss and blocked the exit.

"I don't think so," Scottie shouted back and grabbed his shirt, almost toppling over with the effort. "Sit down or I'll cuff you to the table."

Kevin glared at the detectives. He realized he was overpowered and sat back down on the metal chair with a thud. "Assholes. You can't do this," he murmured.

Gunner was stationed outside the doorway for security. Gibson closed the door and grabbed a chair. After pushing on the recorder, he named the people in the room and asked Kevin if he wanted a lawyer.

"Why? I didn't do anything. I have nothing to say."

"Perhaps so, but I have a great deal to say to you. See if what I have to say fits into a big bag of trouble." Gibson grinned. "Let's begin with where were you on the night your wife was murdered. This time I want the truth."

"I was at work. Like I already…"

"Sea You Later," Gibson interrupted.

"What?" Kevin groaned. "Ah, shit."

"That's right. We know exactly where you were. After ten, anyway. Before ten is another matter."

"I confess. I left work and went to a poker game. So what?" He sneered. His curled lip made his nose scrunch together into an ugly knob.

"Hopkins told us he couldn't give a definite time when you arrived."

"Some of the other guys will know," Kevin whined.

"Well then, I think you'll have to get somebody who can vouch for you. In the meantime, we're going to hold you on suspicion of murder."

"No. You can't do that." Kevin jumped out of his chair.

Scottie stood up again. Even with the cane by her side, her tall, ominous presence was no match for the gangly man. He sat down and gave her a dirty look.

Gibson leaned in toward Kevin. "You had the means and the opportunity. You took the knife from the shed where Dianne had hidden it, didn't you? And it seems as if you come and go from your job unfettered."

"I want a lawyer." Sweat trickled off his forehead.

"Get him a lawyer. And get a blood sample and take his prints." Gibson slammed his fist on the table.

Scottie stopped the recording.

"What about Virginia?" Kevin asked.

"Is there somewhere she could go?" Scottie asked.

"Yeah. Her grandma's house."

"All right. I'll take care of it myself. Get up."

"What now?"

"I have a nice suite just for you. Down the hallway. Not too far from your overnight accommodation." Scottie laughed.

Chapter 35

"Let's get out of here," Gibson said as he stomped out of the room. He had probably had enough for the day. It was getting claustrophobic in the stuffy station. Kevin had added a pungent smell to the interview room with his stale body odour.

"Where to?" Gunner asked.

"I need a coffee." They strolled past an open doorway where two uniformed officers were chatting and joking. The waiting room was empty except for a lady sitting quietly with a small child on her lap. Several phones were ringing in the dispatch room. Gibson ignored everything and headed to the doorway.

"Hey," Grant yelled.

Gibson turned toward the counter.

"Hang on a minute." Grant held up a finger to indicate he wanted a moment with the detective.

Gibson released the door handle. The loud bang reverberated through the lobby. Too tired to do much else, he stood still and waited. Gunner leaned against the wall. Grant uttered a few more words into the phone and hung up.

"I just got a call about a domestic violence incident." He paused. "You're not gonna like this."

"What?" Gibson asked.

"There's a problem at the Parkers'. On Lands End Road."

"At Jackson's house?"

"Yeah. All I know is that someone has a gun," Grant said.

At the mention of a weapon, the DC glanced up.

"I'm sending a couple of patrol cars out. I thought it might have something to do with your case."

"Not sure what's going on. We'll head over there right away," Gibson said.

They hopped into Gunner's vehicle and headed out of town.

"Use your lights and siren," Gibson said. Suddenly he had a very bad feeling about it all.

Gunner was happy to oblige and sped down the highway with blue lights flashing. A whoop, whoop sounded when someone got in his way. He didn't need to ask which house because there were several marked cars blocking a driveway on the waterside.

Gibson flashed his badge at the officer standing guard. The gate was clear along one side so Gunner drove cautiously through the narrow gap. His hands gripped the steering wheel tighter. As they worked their way down the long winding driveway, Gibson's cell rang. He pulled it out of his pocket and peeped at the screen. Not now, he thought. He swiped to ignore the call.

Gunner cruised slowly out of the wooded area and approached the fountain. Behind the splashing water, they could see a red BMW car parked diagonally in front of the garage. The driver's door was open with a man kneeling on the pavement beside it. His hands were above his head. The uncontrolled shaking made his body weave back and forth. His breathing was ragged, his face pallid. He had a harried, wild glint in his eyes that made Gibson think of a coiled rattlesnake. Only a few metres away, a curly-haired lady sat on the bottom step of the porch with a gun aimed at the man's chest. She held the Colt 1911 like it was her friend. It was obvious to Gibson, she was comfortable with the semi-automatic pistol. That made the situation even more dangerous.

Gunner cruised in as close as he could, coming to a halt far enough away as not to be a threat.

The lady looked suspiciously at them.

The man turned at the sound of a vehicle.

Although Gibson realized who they were, he was confused. He opened his car door and stepped out.

"Get this crazy lady away from me," Jackson screeched. His voice was raspy, a tinge of fear on the edges.

The detective crept forward a few steps.

"Halt or I'll blast him right now," Paula said, grinning menacingly.

Gibson stopped abruptly.

"In case you're wondering, I do know how to use it. It's Guy's." She laughed. "He was good for something. Even showed me how to use it."

"Paula. What's going on?"

She waved the gun in the air, pointing over to Gunner for a brief moment. "Tell your buddy there to remain right where he is or..."

Gunner stood by his door. He backed up and held up his hands, palms faced outwards. The blue lights swept over and around them.

Paula kept her arm straight out, never faltering. "It was Jackson."

"Paula. What are you talking about?"

"No, you don't get it. Do you? Take a gander at his broken headlight. I saw his fancy car at the party. I saw him behind the wheel when he ran over my boy. Is everything clear to you now?"

The pain beneath her anger showed in her stiff jaw. She stared at Jackson with cold, hard eyes.

"We'll bring him in for questioning," Gibson said.

Paula turned her gaze toward the detective and shook her head. "I don't think so. He's filthy rich. He'll get away with it."

"I'll make sure..."

"Ryder died a few hours ago."

Gibson lowered his head and rubbed at his temple. Why hadn't someone told him that?

"I've got nothing to live for. If it's over for me, it's over for that scumbag." She had been holding her finger over the trigger. Now she let it rest on the cold steel.

A swoosh sounded as the front door opened. Paula didn't bother to turn, but let out a loud chuckle. "Here comes the faithful wife, coming to save her husband. You're pathetic. He doesn't deserve you, sweetheart."

Mrs. Parker took one step forward and wavered. Gibson shook his head and motioned with his hand for her to move back indoors. Lori glimpsed at Jackson, backed away and shut the door.

"For Christ sake, do something. She's going to kill me," Jackson pleaded.

Gibson was surprised at the wrath of Paula. She had seemed a level-headed woman. Now she was talking like a mad person. He had to find a way to stop her. It had to be something that would resonate with her or she would pull the trigger. He had no doubt of that.

"Is this what you want for Ryder?" Gibson said. "Let me help you."

"For Ryder? He can't feel anything anymore." Paula stroked the trigger gently with her finger.

"Ryder was trying to turn his life around. I think sometimes he felt he was destined to be a criminal like his father. Like Guy. He didn't want to go down that same road. He looked up to you. He was proud that you were his mother," Gibson pleaded, his voice was smoothly professional, although inside his nerves were raw.

"What? A murderer for a mother. That's what I'm going to be."

"It doesn't have to be that way. You could stop now," Gibson said quietly, almost a whisper.

"You need a happy ending, detective?" Paula turned to Gibson. "A fairy tale to tell your children?"

Gibson blanched, but held her gaze. His steel grey eyes softened. He wanted her to get through this. As he watched, her hand lowered a fraction. He almost spoke. He wanted to encourage her with soothing words, but he knew it was better to let her work it out herself.

Paula stared into his grey eyes. She was locked in conflict. A free-fall to the bottom would be easy. It would take courage to hold onto her soul. A tiny flicker sparked as she lowered her gaze. Maybe a thought of her son crossed her mind. She placed the gun on the step gently. Heavy sobs racked her body.

Gibson moved in and picked up the gun. He switched the safety latch on and tucked it into his jacket pocket.

"She tried to kill me. Arrest her," Jackson yelled. He stood up and brushed off his pant legs. The knees were soiled from the wet pavement. "Look at my suit."

Gibson lifted his chin to Gunner.

"Arrest Mr. Parker." He pointed at the BMW. "Have his car towed in for forensics."

"What the hell for?" Jackson sputtered. "I'll have your badge for this."

"Turn around," Gunner said. He slapped on handcuffs and opened the back door of his patrol car. "Watch your head, Mr. Parker."

"You'll pay for this," Jackson shouted.

Gunner closed the door firmly and slid into the driver's seat.

"Catch you later," Gibson said and patted the hood.

The constable accelerated up the driveway and disappeared into the woods. Paula struggled to breathe as she sobbed uncontrollably.

The front door opened again.

"You better get a lawyer for your husband."

Lori turned back inside.

The inspector took out his cell phone and called for a uniformed officer.

"I have to arrest you," Gibson said. He sat next to Paula. "I'm sorry about Ryder."

"I know." She lowered her head and closed her eyes. The tears flowed freely down her cheeks. She didn't try to stop them. Maybe she would never recover from losing him. Perhaps she couldn't.

He wasn't sure what he could do for Paula, but he would try his best. What a bloody mess.

Chapter 36

Bright light washed across Gibson's face. He opened one eye and looked over to the other side of the bed. Katherine was already gone. He sat up and stretched. His cell phone beeped on the other side of the room. The clock clicked over, showing him it was already after ten. How had he managed to sleep so long? He sprang out of bed and plucked up his cell. Six calls missed. All from Scottie.

Gibson stripped and headed straight for the shower. He leaned against the tiles and let the hot beads of water pummel his weary body. His body ached through and through. As he stood in front of the mirror, he examined his scruffy face. He shaved, and then reached into the medicine cabinet to find some pain pills. The bottle was missing. It was likely in Katherine's nightstand. He unlocked the drawer and stopped dead. There was an envelope with his name scrawled on the top. He plucked it up and fingered it, thinking about what it could be.

"Katherine. Are you there?" Gibson yelled out. He went to the bedroom door and shouted down the hallway. "Katherine."

Only eerie silence answered.

Gibson sat on the bed and opened the letter.

Dear William, by the time you read this I will be in the air somewhere over Alberta. Rather, you are so obsessed with your cases, especially this one, that I have probably landed in Ontario.

Katherine.

Gibson clasped his mouth in shock. He stayed there for several minutes trying to decide what to do. A cold fear gripped his heart. He ran to the kitchen, but Katherine wasn't there. He headed out the back door and went into the greenhouse. Nothing. A wave of nausea made his head spin. He grabbed onto the counter loaded with trays of herbs. The heady scent of basil floated in the air. He sucked in his breath. He would miss this. Katherine's space. Where could she be? Had she already left him?

He dashed back into the house and into the bedroom, checking the closet. Nothing was missing that he could tell. Gibson sat back on the bed, the letter still clutched in his hand. The fear had a firm hold of him now. Katherine put colour into his darkness. He had brought all of this upon himself with his actions. Saying sorry hadn't been enough.

Gibson started at the creak of the back door. Then gurgling noises from the coffee maker floated down the hall. He bolted into the kitchen—Katherine stood there in her flawed perfection.

"Good morning, sleepy," she said. A girlish grin appeared, and then faded when she saw the letter in his hand.

"Are you leaving me?"

"What? No. Never." Katherine rushed over to him.

"But this..." Gibson waved the envelope.

"You weren't supposed to see that. I was simply letting go of my demons. I should have pitched it away." She stroked his cheek. "I'm sorry."

Gibson's cell rang.

"You better answer that. I'll pour you a coffee."

"Gibson." He listened to Scottie for several minutes before hanging up.

Katherine looked at him from across the room. His lips were compressed into a frown.

"More bad news?" she asked.

"Maybe." He paused. "I have to go."

Katherine pushed a lock of hair behind her ear.

"We'll be fine. I promise." Gibson pulled her in tight and held onto her for what felt like an eternity. The heat of her body provided strength to him. He had been in a daze for most of the week, with lack of sleep and worry. Immediately he felt a semblance of ease. They moved apart. He kissed her on the cheek, inhaling the scent of her hair.

"You better get going." Katherine laughed.

Gibson hurried to get ready. He grabbed his gun and badge, thinking maybe this would be his final case.

* * *

As he drove down the highway, his phone rang.

"Gibson."

"I got a call from Jackson's attorney. They're not very happy," Rex said.

"Well, they're going to be even more unhappy when I finish with him," he replied to the police chief.

"Is he under arrest?"

"Yes."

"That's too bad. I actually quite admire the guy. He does a lot for the community," Rex said.

"I know. He made a grave mistake with this," Gibson replied. He thought about Anatoe and the fundraiser and how all of this would affect him.

"Well, keep me posted…" Rex paused.

Gibson wasn't confident the chief was still on the line. He strained to hear anything. Then Rex's booming voice blasted him. He pulled the phone away from his ear.

"What about the murder down at the pier? Any progress there?"

"Yes. We have a suspect in custody. We'll get the forensics quite soon and hopefully wrap that one up."

"Excellent." Rex hung up.

Gibson turned right at the light and headed down Beacon Avenue. A couple more turns took him to the station. He parked in the lot and rushed indoors. The regular desk sergeant was back on duty. Gibson surveyed a gentleman in a dark navy suit sitting on the hard bench. He jumped up when he observed the detective.

"I'm Jackson's attorney. Lester Moore. Are you Gibson?"

"Yes."

"I've spoken to Rex," the attorney stated.

"Yes, I know."

"Well. Are you going to release my client?"

"No. I'm afraid not," Gibson said.

"What? You can't keep him forever."

"Right. We just got back the results from forensics. I intend to interview Mr. Parker later this morning, and then–"

"Time is running out." The lawyer snapped and tapped at his Rolex. "He's been in that deplorable cell for way too long. It's an absolute outrage. I intend to put in a formal complaint against you. Against the whole station."

"So be it." Gibson walked away.

"Where the hell are you going now?" Lester asked.

"I have some urgent things to attend to first," Gibson said. He moved around to the counter, hiding the smirk on his face.

"Bloody hell." The lawyer stormed out of the building, his cell phone pressed to his ear.

"Oh my," the desk sergeant said. "Scottie's waiting. Watch out, though. She's steaming mad at you." He peeked at the clock on the wall behind him. "She's been here for several hours."

"Yeah, yeah. Everybody wants a piece." Gibson rushed down the corridor. He swung open the door to the interview room.

Scottie sat slumped in her chair, earbuds attached to her phone. Gibson could hear the music clearly. How her ears must hum. She sat upright and ripped the cord away. "I've been trying to get to you all morning."

"I know." Gibson sat opposite. He propped his elbows on the table and placed his head in his hands. "Sorry. I'm here now."

"So, a lot has gone on. I don't know where to start." Scottie crossed her arms. "The forensics on Kevin isn't looking good for us. The partial print isn't his. I'm just waiting on the DNA. Should be soon." She frowned.

"Will the partial print identify anyone?" Gibson asked, doubting it would. It wasn't clear enough to decipher.

"Jocko says probably not."

"All right. So, we're counting on the blood matching."

"That's right. The blood found on the knife has to be Kevin's or we're hooped. We have no witnesses." Scottie glanced over to her partner. "Sorry about Ryder."

"Yeah, me too."

Scottie's phone vibrated along the table. She grabbed it and peered at the screen. "Here it is."

Gibson leaned in closer to hear what Jocko had to say.

"Scottie here." She nodded several times quickly. Her mouth twitched as she gnawed on the inside of her cheek. "Really. That's it." She hung up and shook her head.

"Damn. If it's not Kevin, then who? Was Jocko positive?"

"It's not Kevin," Scottie said tightly. She put her phone down and tapped on it. "Where do we go from here?"

"God damn it." Gibson repeated. "Better get the paperwork done. Call his lawyer and get him out of here." He was so mad, he wished he could charge Kevin with domestic abuse. But that train had left the station.

"Okay." Scottie knew exactly what her boss was thinking. She had never seen him so incensed. His face had gone red.

"Hey, Scottie. How did Paula make out in court this morning?" Gibson needed to think about something else. He took a deep breath. If he could slug the guy and get away with it, he would. Better to concentrate on things that mattered.

"Your lawyer friend got her bail."

"That's a good start. Deb is a tiger. She has experience defending firearms charges. And she's very successful at minimizing the charges."

"Anatoe was there, too."

"Oh."

"He sat beside Paula for support. Held her hand."

"He's a great kid. Well, I guess he's all grown up now. Anatoe will be a loyal friend for her." Gibson grinned.

"Crown counsel has elected to proceed by summary conviction for pointing a firearm at someone. She could have been indicted for her actions, but they took the extenuating circumstances of her son's death into account. And she has no priors." Scottie gave him a small smile.

"That's a good break. What about having possession of an illegal firearm?"

"The gun is actually registered in her name."

"Wow!" People never failed to amaze Gibson. There was nothing more they could do for Paula, although he would be a character witness for her if necessary. He supposed Anatoe would be, as well. Yes, Paula had some good friends to lean on. That made him feel a tiny bit better. "Well, that's that, then."

"The gun wasn't loaded," Scottie said.

"Oh. Jesus. I almost can't blame Paula for doing what she did," Gibson said. He left the rest unspoken. Losing a child. A part of him felt a little of her pain, just from what had happened with Katherine. He sighed heavily. Not at all the same, really. Unfathomable.

"I hear you." Scottie nodded her head. She stared at Gibson and smiled.

"Jackson's lawyer was waiting in the lobby when I got here."

"We'll have to tackle him next." Her lips stretched out to form a straight line like she had a secret.

Gibson figured she had already taken a long hard look at the forensics. Guilty.

Chapter 37

Jackson's lawyer wasn't in the lobby. He hadn't left a message with the desk sergeant either, so the detectives went out for something to eat. They walked down Beacon Avenue to a popular bistro. The lunch crowd had come and gone with a few stragglers left behind having a second cup of coffee. They seized the best table by the window. The waitress was a young university student who bounced over to them before they had even sat down. She wore a black outfit with a white apron tied in the back into a giant bow. Her braided hair reached almost to her waistline. She batted her lashes as she accepted their order, probably vying for a good tip to enhance her meagre student loan.

The espresso machine was loud enough to put all conversation on pause. Gibson inhaled the smell of fresh ground beans. Within minutes, the cute waitress served up two lattes with a rosette design in the milky froth. The detectives sat back and enjoyed the piping hot drink.

"The forensics team did a tremendous job yesterday," Scottie said. "They found bits of glass on the road in front of Paula's house."

"From a headlight?"

Scottie raised an eyebrow and took another sip of her beverage.

"Did the pieces match up with the cracked lens on Jackson's BMW?" Gibson asked.

"Absolutely. No question at all," Scottie said. "And not only that, but Ryder's bike had paint on the back fender from the impact."

"Red paint?"

"You know it. BMW red paint."

"Then what are we waiting for?"

"My burger." She giggled.

The food was delivered pronto. As they ate, Gibson couldn't stop thinking about Dianne, and how they had failed her.

"What was Jackson doing on that street anyway?"

"I don't know. That did strike me as kind of weird." Scottie took a bite of her burger. "And why would he leave his own party?"

"I left the party early, so I don't know how long it went on for."

"Still, why that street?" Scottie asked. She stared at her partner.

They sat in silence for a long moment.

"Something isn't right here." Gibson said. He thought for a moment. "What if he ran Ryder over on purpose?"

"What the hell?"

"Ryder was trying to tell me something on the night of the fundraiser. I couldn't make it out at the time, and Katherine had fallen ill, but I think he may have identified the killer at the party. I guess I've been looking at this upside down. Both Chelsea and Hudson said Dianne was having an affair. I thought Kevin had found out and killed her. But Kevin is in the clear. So, was it the other way around? Was it Jackson who killed her?"

"Wait a minute… did Ryder recognize Jackson as the man from the pier? Is that what you're saying?" Scottie asked.

"It's the only thing that makes any sense now with everything else that has happened," Gibson said. "I can't see any other reason why Jackson would want to run over Ryder. It couldn't possibly be just a coincidence. That's not feasible."

"Oh, crap. Dianne was pregnant. Was it Jackson's? Could she have confronted him with that?"

Suddenly Gibson felt ill. Was he to blame for Ryder's death? If he had only listened to the boy, would he still be alive?

"You're not to blame, Gibson." Scottie knew his thought process and reached out. "Jackson is the bad guy here."

"I just can't stop thinking about it now." Gibson shook his head.

"Let's go get him," Scottie said, although they didn't have any proof. Not quite yet anyway.

They abandoned their meal and hurried back to the station as quick as one can with a cane. Jackson's wife sat quietly on the bench where the lawyer had waited earlier. No tears had spoiled her makeup. She had on a short-sleeved blouse over a navy pencil skirt. Her diamond jewellery didn't sparkle in the fluorescent lights of the lobby. She stared at the stains on the linoleum floor. Her nose was pushed up to shut out the stench, and her mouth was clamped shut. She looked up at the sound of the door opening, then gazed back down.

Lester Moore paced in front of the counter, spouting out at the desk sergeant at every chance. "Where the hell are they now? I won't tolerate this."

"Sorry to keep you waiting," Gibson said. "Shall we go to an interview room?"

"Fine." Lester picked up the briefcase that had fallen off the bench. He turned back to Lori. "You should wait here until Jackson gets released."

"All right."

They headed down the hallway to the nice room. The detectives sat on the far side. Lester sat rod straight in the first chair. He put his briefcase on the seat adjacent to him and sorted out some papers. After flipping through several pages, he put one sheet on the table along with a pen. Shouting from the back cells made him look up. Jackson appeared in the doorway. His wrinkled suit hung loose over his bent-over figure.

"What the hell took you so long," Jackson yelled at his lawyer. "Get me out of this frigging place."

"Have a seat, Mr. Parker," Scottie said. She pointed to the chair next to the recorder. With a stab, she pressed it on and announced who was present.

"All right. The glass collected at the scene of the accident matched the broken lens on your vehicle. The red BMW." Gibson tapped at a report in front of him and rambled off the license plate. "That's you. Correct?"

Jackson stared at his lawyer.

"You can answer the question."

"Yes. That's my car, but..."

Lester laid a hand on his client's arm to stop him from saying any more.

"Why didn't you stop?" Gibson asked.

"How many times do I have to tell you, it wasn't me. I wasn't there and I didn't run over anybody," Jackson spewed out in a blur of words.

"You actually want us to believe you could hit a person and not know it?" Gibson persisted.

"It wasn't me." Jackson sat back in his chair and crossed his arms.

"What were you doing on that particular street?" Scottie asked. She could barely keep her anger in check.

"What is your problem?" Jackson turned to his lawyer. "Do something!"

"Detective, Mr. Parker was not involved in the hit and run."

"We have proof it was your vehicle," Gibson said, ignoring both men.

"That's not possible. I was at my party. As anyone there can tell you…" Jackson stopped.

"I think we better get to the court for the bail hearing," Lester said. "We have nothing more to say on the matter." He stuffed the paper and pen in his briefcase and pushed his chair back.

Gibson turned to Scottie. She shook her head again.

"Well?" Lester tapped his knuckles on the table.

Gibson's cell pinged. "Give me a moment." He jumped up and hurried out of the room.

Scottie turned off the recorder and sat back in her chair. She gazed at the ceiling to ward off the hateful glare from Jackson.

It was quite a while before Gibson returned. He closed the door quietly behind him.

"This is an outrage. A travesty of justice," Lester said. He jumped up quickly.

"Enough with the fancy talk. Sit down, Mr. Moore," Gibson said. He didn't hold back his disgust. "Your client is in serious trouble."

"The courts will decide that, detective," Lester shot back and sat.

Gibson gestured to Scottie. She turned the tape recorder on again.

"Mr. Jackson Parker, you are under arrest for the murder of Dianne Meadows…"

"This is bullshit," Jackson screamed. He slammed his fist down on the table.

"You have no evidence of that," Lester said.

Gibson finished reading Jackson his rights before he responded. "The forensics team found blood on the stick shift of the BMW that matches the victim."

"That only proves Dianne was in his car," Lester said. "She cut herself."

"Why was she in the car?"

"We went to meetings together. Sometimes I drove," Jackson butted in. He gazed at his attorney. "Sort this out now, Lester."

"If that is all you have, these charges are not warranted."

"I will decide that. We believe the blood dripped off his sleeve after killing Dianne. You didn't wipe your car interior clean enough," Gibson said. "Furthermore, we believe you followed Ryder with the explicit intent to kill him because he saw you at the crime scene and then identified you at the party."

"You have no proof of any of this," Lester said. "It's all circumstantial."

"We have a search warrant for your house," Gibson said. He peered over to Scottie. She slapped handcuffs on Jackson and led him out.

"Lester. Do something," he called as the detective steered him back to his tiny cubicle.

"I will. Don't say anything to anybody," Lester yelled. He gathered his belongings and headed for the lobby. After a few words with Lori, he left the building.

Mrs. Parker stood up and followed the lawyer out.

Gibson leaned back in his chair, wondering where to go from here. He had jumped the gun like he always did. Jocko had run the blood that was found on the stick shift. At the time, the detectives hadn't connected the accident with Dianne's murder, so Jackson's DNA hadn't been checked with that found on the murder weapon. It was only a few hours ago that they had any inkling Jackson was involved with her death. They would have to be hopeful while they waited for the results. Perhaps the house search would uncover some evidence. A bloody suit would do fine.

Gibson closed his eyes briefly.

Chapter 38

Dawn arrived with the chirping of birds and a patter of rainfall on the windowpane. Gibson peeped over to Katherine and slipped out of bed. He headed to the kitchen and switched on the coffee maker. After a quick shower and shave, he checked his cell phone. Nothing yet from Jocko. And Scottie wasn't answering her cell. Why hadn't she phoned him about the house search?

Katherine walked into the room and sat at the table. She wore a plain black dress and red pumps. Her hair was pinned up in the back.

"What a depressing day it's going to be," Gibson said.

"Poor Paula." Katherine looked outside to the dark clouds that gave a greyish sheen to the light. A breeze rustled the leaves of the trees and brought a taste of the sea with it. "Is it going to rain all day?"

"It's letting up already," Gibson said. He viewed the clock over the sink. "Nearly time to go."

Katherine gave him the faintest of smiles.

Gibson took the back roads to the funeral home. The parking lot was completely full. Vehicles were parked down the narrow lane as far as he could see.

"I'll drop you off and park."

"I'll wait in front."

Gibson left his cell in the truck and trudged back to the stone building. Although the rain had stopped, there were large puddles on the road. He skipped over them to avoid getting soaked. Katherine stood by the doors clutching her handbag. Her hickory brown eyes were heavy with unwept tears. Gibson took her by the hand. They stepped inside to a big room with delicate lighting and wood-paneled walls. The air was perfumed by the sweet scent of roses. Soft piano music played in the background. The rows of chairs, most of which were filled, were crowded together, leaving little room to manoeuvre. A large group of teenagers stood at the back, speaking in hushed tones. Anatoe sat in the front row with Paula. She hung onto his arm as if she would never let him go.

Gibson and his wife moved up the aisle and sat in the empty seats saved for them. The coffin next to the pulpit was dark mahogany, perfectly polished. It was the only thing Gibson saw. Once again, his heart twisted in his chest. The sense of failure washed over him. It was very hard not to cry. But was it for his failings or for Ryder? He sighed deeply and squeezed Katherine's hand. She rubbed his shoulder, knowing guilt was eating him up.

The ceremony was short and simple. A family friend said a few words. Quiet weeping swept over the assembly. Paula sat in still sorrow. Anatoe lowered his head, lost in thought.

Afterward, most people left quietly. A few close friends and family headed down the stone walkway to the gravesite. Gibson watched as Paula leaned into the tall, strong frame of her new-found friend. Anatoe opened the wrought iron gate and directed them to the far corner. The well-tended grounds belied the mood of the visitors. Gibson spun away. He clung on to Katherine, afraid if he let go, he would go down into a dark abyss. How the tables had turned. At one time he had been the rock. For the first time, he recognised that love was a two-way street. He felt a deep gratitude for the bond that held them together.

"Let's go for lunch," Katherine said lightly. Her intuition was insightful.

"There's a real nice bistro in Sidney."

* * *

On the way into town, Gibson's cell rang. Hesitant to lose the moment, he disregarded the call. Katherine turned the volume on the radio up and slunk back into her seat. He pulled onto Beacon Avenue and cruised down toward the waterfront. It was an extremely busy Saturday morning. Street parking was virtually impossible on the main drag, so he drove up and down the side streets until an empty spot appeared. The walk back to the bistro was pleasant with a fresh smell in the air that came after an August shower. The restaurant was thinning out as the lunch hour was already past its peak time. From the window seats, they took in the hordes of people strolling past, relishing the sun and the last of the summer days. They barely spoke through their meal, happy to be in each other's company. The events of the morning had been heartbreaking, and needed to be left behind so that they could move forward. But Gibson knew he had to get back to work soon. He started to explain, but Katherine cut him off.

"That was lovely. I should get home," she said. "You have things to do."

They walked along the path by the shoreline, the long way back to where the truck was parked. The sky reflecting on the water made the landscape blend together, only broken by the brightly-coloured spinnakers dotting the azure blue sea. The sailboats glided through the waves, pushed by the light breeze blowing down the strait. In the distance, a line of boats were anchored along the length of the sand spit. Other, more adventurous, boaters zipped by in their cabin cruisers with destinations of nearby islands to explore.

Gibson cruised home by the back streets to avoid the heavy traffic on the highway. He pulled into the driveway and shut off the engine. Katherine leaned in, their foreheads touching. Her lips brushed his as she pushed off. At the front door, she waved before she stepped inside. Gibson backed out onto the lane. He caught a glimpse of sparkling water between two buildings. It beckoned him over. Instead, he picked up his cell and called Scottie, unaware of the troubles ahead.

"I'm at the lab with Jocko," Scottie said.

"Be right there."

It was quiet in the lobby. When Gibson entered the forensics lab, Scottie and the forensic scientist were seated on tall stools in front of a monitor. They both glanced up at the sound of the door opening.

"Hi," Scottie said.

"Did you uncover anything at the house?" Gibson asked.

"Nothing."

Gibson remained silent. He looked at Jocko. "Did the partial print give us anything?"

"Like I said before. It wasn't a good specimen," the technician said.

"What about DNA on the knife?"

"It should be any minute now," Scottie said.

The sound of a printer resounded loudly in the quiet room. Jocko headed to the corner. He bent over a counter with his back to them. Soon, he turned around and held up a slip of paper.

"I think this is what you were waiting for." He strolled across the room and handed the results of the DNA test to the inspector. His face held no clue to the outcome.

"We have a problem," Gibson said as he stared at the paper.

Chapter 39

Although it was late, the detectives hauled their asses upstairs to Gibson's office to sort out the conflicting evidence. Gibson sat at his desk with his feet propped up on the bottom drawer and put in a call to Paula. After speaking briefly with her, he hung up and sat back to think some more. As he mulled over the facts, he remembered the memory stick of the wine store CCTV footage and decided to take a look for himself. After rummaging through the top compartment where he had tossed it earlier, he found it among the paper clips and pens. He plugged it into his laptop and hit the rewind button.

Gibson stared at the screen, his eyes blurring as suit after suit went into the store and out again. Then, something caught his eye, something everyone had missed the first time around. Probably because it was unexpected. Not a suit and not a kid. He paused the video, rewound a few minutes back and watched again.

Meanwhile, Scottie phoned Lester Moore to set up a meeting in the interview room at the RCMP station in two hours. Earlier in the day, she had asked the lawyer if his client was ready to talk to them. Lester had passed on a message from Jackson to tell her to go to hell. She hung up the phone and frowned.

"He wasn't very nice."

"No doubt," Gibson replied. "Take a look at this." He pointed to the screen.

Scottie stood behind him and watched the video. "Well, well. Is that who I think it is?"

"I believe so."

"Should I get Gunner on it?"

"Absolutely."

The detectives made their way to the lobby and out of the building. They hopped into the F150 truck and worked their way out of the city. Once on the highway, Gibson put a lead foot on the gas pedal. As he closed in on Sidney, he switched to the slow lane and turned right at the light. A short while later, he pulled into the RCMP station.

Grant was at the desk once more. He shrugged helplessly. "We're short of staff. Holidays." He pointed to the back. "Same room. Everything is arranged as per your instructions."

Gibson nodded.

Scottie smirked.

The detectives glanced at Mrs. Parker sitting on the bench as they walked past her and headed down the hallway. They could hear arguing coming from the room. Gibson strolled in without knocking and sat in the same chair as the other day. Jackson scowled at him. Scottie sat and turned on the recorder.

Lester Moore had his briefcase on the chair next to him. He sat with his hands laced together on the table. His dark suit had thin red stripes that were barely noticeable. He wore his tie knotted up tight to his neck. His face seemed relaxed, nearly smiling.

Jackson sagged in his chair. He wore an official uniform of orange. The colour clashed with his yellowish skin. The bags under his eyes were dark from lack of sleep. Something flashed beneath the surface of his hardened stare. Revenge? Hatred? Gibson wasn't really sure. Now that he was here in this room, all he could think about was leaving. Another glimpse toward the prisoner made him believe Jackson was likely thinking the same.

Somebody was talking. Gibson flinched when Scottie touched his hand.

"My client wants to make a statement about Dianne," Lester said.

Gibson sat back in his chair and tried to concentrate on what was being said. He hadn't been expecting Jackson to say anything. They were here to tell him things.

He turned to Jackson. "Go ahead."

"Dianne and I had been seeing each other."

"You mean having an affair," Scottie said.

"Yes, if that makes you happy," he replied with a snarky tone. He glimpsed over to his attorney. Lester had lowered his head and was staring at the floor.

Scottie's cell rang. She looked at the screen and left the room.

"Go on," Gibson encouraged.

"Dianne said she had something important to tell me. We had stopped the affair weeks before, so I was reluctant to talk to her." He paused. "We never said much at work, in case someone caught us. I agreed to meet her down by the pier that night." Jackson swallowed with difficulty. "I was stunned when she told me she was pregnant. I had been very cautious. I didn't believe it was mine. I told her that, too. That started a yelling match. Then, she went nuts and pulled out a knife. I was shocked. I didn't know what was going on. Then, she started to brandish it around. I tried to calm her down, but she wasn't having it. I really thought she was going to stab me, so I ran and got the hell out of there. But I swear she was alive when I left." He broke off.

Scottie quietly returned and sat down. She gave Gibson a nod.

"We ran your DNA against the blood found on the murder weapon…"

"No way." Jackson jumped out of his chair.

"It wasn't a match. We know you didn't kill Dianne. But all of this begs the question of who was driving your car?"

A silence came over them. Jackson sat back down and glanced at his lawyer.

"It wasn't you. You would have no reason to harm Ryder. Isn't that true?" Gibson said. He already knew the answer to this, after having spoken with Paula. She had only assumed it was Jackson driving the BMW and admitted she hadn't seen the driver. She only knew it was his car, and that had been enough to convince her of his guilt and point the finger at him.

The quietness grew deeper.

Scottie spoke up. "There is only one other person who had access to your vehicle."

"I don't know what you're talking about," Jackson replied.

"Come off it."

"Maybe someone took it for a joy ride."

"Oh, really. Get real. Your wife was driving the car," Scottie barked.

"I didn't know."

"Of course, you did." Scottie slammed the table.

Gibson held up his hand. "We have arrested your wife," he said solemnly.

"What?" Jackson glanced at his lawyer again.

Lester shook his head.

"I'm sure it was just an accident," Jackson said, still in denial of what was happening.

"We've arrested her for the murder of Dianne Meadows."

"Lori? She's been arrested for murder?" Jackson placed his head in his hands and moaned. He looked up at the detective. "She knew about us? I mean, Dianne and me."

"Apparently so," Gibson agreed. People made him so mad. Was that all he cared about? Getting caught cheating. What about Ryder? What was his life worth?

"How many times?" Scottie asked.

"What?" Jackson turned to her.

"How many times did you cheat on your wife? How many different women?"

Jackson's face contorted, his lips quivered. It was the face of a man who realized he had pushed his wife over the edge.

"I guess Lori finally reached her tolerance threshold," Scottie sneered.

"What will happen to me now?"

"You are free to go. But Lori won't be seeing the light of day anytime soon. You better get her a lawyer." Gibson gestured to Scottie. She pushed the recorder off.

Jackson opened his mouth, but no words came out. Just a whoosh of air.

Lester gathered his papers together quickly and swung open the door. They could hear a commotion coming from the cell area.

"You bastard! You've ruined my life. Couldn't keep it in your pants, could you?" Lori screamed. "Can you hear me, Jackson? I should have killed you instead."

Jackson glanced back at Gibson momentarily before he sprinted down the hallway to the front entrance with Lester on his heels.

Gibson shut the door to muffle the increasingly ear-splitting and obnoxious rant coming from the enraged woman. They sat for a while before he spoke.

"So we got Lori on the security camera tape heading toward the pier. That's good," Gibson said. "Tell me Gunner found the dress she was wearing."

"Yeah, he found it straight away. The large floral pattern was quite distinct. It was hanging in the laundry room. It had been washed, but we all know there will be traces of blood on it still."

Gibson nodded his head in agreement.

"Jocko is working on the dress as we speak."

"What about the blood on the knife? Do we know if it's Lori's DNA?"

"Well, Grant arrested Lori after we went into the interview room just as we had arranged with him. He got a DNA sample from her and sent it over to the lab immediately. We should get that any minute now."

As if the gods were listening, Scottie's cell phone rang. She hung up after a few minutes.

"Well?"

"Jocko used the rapid DNA testing and has confirmed it's Lori's blood lodged in the hilt of the knife."

"Great. That's the evidence we need."

"Yup."

"So Lori followed her husband to the pier, although he left before she could confront him. But unfortunately, Dianne was still there," Gibson said.

"That is the logical sequence of events."

"Lori would have been seeing red by then."

"Oh, yeah," Scottie said.

"I suppose she had known that Jackson was the cheating husband all along and finally cracked." Gibson drew in a deep breath. "We'll get the full story in time. At least, Lori's version of the truth. But I think the ladies got into a scuffle and Dianne came out the loser."

"Why did Dianne take the knife with her? She would still be alive if she hadn't," Scottie said.

"Maybe she was afraid of going down there at night. Remember she told Constable Grant that she suspected the street kids were involved in the robberies. And, the pier is close to the hostel." Gibson shrugged and let out a sigh.

"I guess, we'll never really know."

"It was a stupid thing to do," Gibson added.

"Lori must have been relieved when we picked up Ryder, thinking she was home free," Scottie said, then frowned. "But Gibson, why did she run him over?"

"She probably heard the confrontation on the terrace between her husband and Ryder. Then the kid runs to me. In her mind, she may have thought that Jackson was going to go down for the murder. The jig was up. She couldn't let that happen. I think Lori's worst fear was losing her status, the security of wealth and all it entails."

"I get it. Lori wasn't going to let anything destroy her life. Her cushy life with the big house, fancy jewels and all that," Scottie said. "The kid was just another obstacle."

"Yeah. That's about it."

"We'll get all the particulars when we interview her tomorrow. One thing I know for sure, she's going to be behind bars for a long time."

"Let's get out of here," Gibson said. He had one more thing to do before heading home.

Chapter 40

Gibson stood by the window in his office. The Olympic Mountains gleamed white on their rugged peaks. Even in summer, the snow persisted. It was a sight he never tired of. The water in the straits below was shrouded in a low fog—autumn was getting ready to rush in as the days got shorter. He watched the horizon as oranges and reds crept across the indigo sky before the sun plunged below the hills. The coppery hues gave way to twilight, where Gibson had been living for the past year. Now that was over; he had made his decision.

The efficient hum of diesel engines of a cruise ship reverberated in the windless air. Then a thousand lights several storeys high came into view. Gibson returned to his desk and slumped into the lush leather. He drew open the top drawer and pulled out the letter he had written weeks before. It felt like a long time ago. So much had happened since. So many terrible things. He set those thoughts aside and tried to think of the good. There was his son, Anatoe, who had come into his life unexpectedly. He was a kind and thoughtful man born from a long-gone love in another lifetime. Paula had lost her only son, but she would find solace in the blossoming friendship with

Anatoe. Although he and Katherine suffered a loss too, they had each other. Better than ever before. Gibson had ultimately realized their connection was strong.

He heard footsteps tapping across the marble floors and swivelled toward the doorway. Scottie stood on the threshold and gazed at the letter on the desk. She walked to the window and watched a ship pull into the port. Ropes were thrown onto the dock and quickly whipped around large metal cleats bolted through the massive timbers.

"Is this it, then?" Scottie asked as she twisted round to face him. "Are you sure?"

"Yes. Absolutely."

"Does Katherine know?"

"I haven't told her, but she knows."

"Yes, she would. She knows you too well," Scottie said. She crossed the room and sat in the chair across from Gibson.

"I'll miss you."

"You know where I live."

"Who will be our boss now?"

"I don't know, Scottie." Gibson picked up the letter and struck it on the desk. "I wanted to tell you before submitting my resignation officially."

"What will you do?" She stared into his grey eyes.

"I plan to hang out with Katherine first," he answered. "Then, it is possible Anatoe will need some help in his garage."

"Really?" Scottie laughed, heartier than ever.

"Katherine said I was skilled with a wrench." Gibson smirked.

"She only sees the best in you."

"That's undeniably true." Gibson lowered his head just for one moment, for the wrongs he had done. All of that was in the past. Katherine had probably suspected, but... he let that thought pass. He would wholly live his life from now on.

Scottie reached over the desk. They shook hands firmly.

"I'll catch you later. I have an appointment." Gibson wasn't certain if Rex would be surprised or not. The police chief's ability to see through people was uncanny. He stood up slowly. At the door, he twisted round and took a final look at his office.

"Good luck, Gibson." Scottie laughed. She had finally gotten in the last word.

If you enjoyed this book, please let others know by leaving a quick review on Amazon. Also, if you spot anything untoward in the paperback, get in touch. We strive for the best quality and appreciate reader feedback.

editor@thebookfolks.com

Other titles by Kathy Garthwaite

In this series:

Murder on Vancouver Island (Book 1)
Murder at Lake Ontario (Book 2)

The Detective Marlowe Flint series:

Sign up to our mailing list to find out about new releases and special offers!

www.thebookfolks.com

Printed in Great Britain
by Amazon